THE Balfour LEGACY

Mia's Scandal
MICHELLE REID

M&B™ and M&B™ with the Rose Device
are trademarks of the publisher.
Harlequin Mills & Boon Limited, Eton House,
18-24 Paradise Road, Richmond, Surrey TW9 1SR

MIA'S SCANDAL © by Harlequin Books SA 2010

Special thanks and acknowledgement are given to Michelle Reid for
her contribution to The Balfour Legacy series

ISBN: 978 0 263 87058 9

053-0710

Harlequin Mills & Boon policy is to use papers that are
natural, renewable and recyclable products and made from
wood grown in sustainable forests. The logging and
manufacturing processes conform to the legal environmental
regulations of the country of origin.

Printed and bound in Spain
by Litografia Rosés S.A., Barcelona

041121126

Michelle Reid grew up on the southern edges of Manchester, the youngest in a family of five lively children. Now she lives in the beautiful county of Cheshire, with her busy executive husband and two grown-up daughters. She loves reading, the ballet and playing tennis when she gets the chance. She hates cooking, cleaning and despises ironing! Sleep she can do without and produces some of her best written work during the early hours of the morning.

For Imelda, my wonderful mother, who is
currently enjoying her ninety-ninth year.
Thanks, Mum, for gifting me with my love of
reading and encouraging me to dare to write.

PROLOGUE

MIA stood poised between two great stone gateposts on top of which stood a matching pair of fierce golden griffins perched as if ready to swoop.

A fine shiver ran down her taut backbone. She had to drag her eyes away from their watchful presence in case they glared her into losing her nerve. Part eagle, part lion, she recognised the two fearsome creatures from the Balfour family crest she'd seen emblazoned on the Balfour website along with the family motto *Validus, Superbus quod Fidelis...*

Powerful, Proud and Loyal...

'*Dio,*' she breathed in a soft shaken whisper, so intimidated by the sheer opulent grandeur of the stately entrance that the butterflies already playing havoc in her stomach went wild.

Behind her, the sound of the taxicab that had brought her here from the airport was slowly fading into the distance, leaving her alone in the weak February sunlight filtering down through the bare branches of the overhanging trees.

It felt strange to think that only one short week ago she had been living her life with her aunt in rural Tuscany, completely unaware that there was a rich and glamorous English family called Balfour, never mind that she could be connected to the glorious name.

She would *still* be unaware of it if that coldly distant person who was supposed to be her mother had not ignored her pleas to let her come and visit her, making Tia Giulia decide it was time to reveal a dark secret she had been keeping to herself for twenty long years.

Now here she stood on the very brink of meeting Oscar Balfour. Proud head of the house of Balfour. Powerful businessman and billion-aire. Husband to three very different wives and father to seven—*seven*—beautiful daughters.

Eight daughters, Mia adjusted, and it made her tummy flip over.

Would a man who had already been blessed with seven daughters want another one?

It was the question she had come all this way to ask him. She needed to face Oscar Balfour and take his reaction to her existence square on her vulnerable chin. If he refused to acknowledge her, then what had she lost but a little bit more of her heart? The cold rejection of her mother had clawed out another huge chunk of it, so his rejection could not be any more hurtful, could it?

And anyway, there was that chance that he might be prepared to welcome her.

Biting down on her full soft trembling lip, Mia reached down to grasp the handle of her suitcase, then straightened. Setting her narrow shoulders inside her soft woven jacket she tipped the case onto its wheels. Her heart was going pitter-patter, she noticed, feeling a tightening across her chest that made it almost impossible for her to breathe. As she stepped out and placed her weight on her leading foot, tiny pinpricks of tension tingled up her leg to her spine. For a second she felt slightly dizzy. For a second she had to close her eyes.

When she opened them again she found she was staring down a long stretch of driveway lined either side by an avenue of old trees. She could not see the house from here because of a dip in the land ahead, but she knew it was out there defending its privacy in its own secluded valley, because it had said so on the Balfour website.

Now all she had to do was walk between those two lines of trees towards it, she told herself, aware as she made herself start walking that her insides were truly quailing with dread at what she was doing, and yet also aware of a quivering, tumbling sense of excitement that danced like fire in her blood.

Nikos Theakis was not a man who suffered emotional excesses. In fact, he prided himself on his cold, calm businesslike approach to most facets of his life. But as he drove away from his breakfast meeting with Oscar that morning, there was nothing calm or businesslike about what he was taking away with him.

He was in shock. The whole Balfour family was in shock, the only one of them seemingly managing to cope being Lillian Balfour herself.

A soft curse broke free from his throat as the pale frail image of Oscar's beautiful wife swam up in front of him, smiling bravely as she'd bid him a painfully final farewell.

Emotion swooped down through his body, sending his foot down hard on the accelerator as if the angry burst of speed would take the alien feeling away. The powerful car leapt forward, up and out of the valley, taking him beneath the canopy of tangling bare branches that lined his route away from the Balfour estate.

But he wasn't concentrating. Nikos knew that even as he saw her standing there, directly in his way. For a few chilling seconds he was so sure he was seeing some ghostly apparition dressed all in black that he forgot to slam his foot on the brakes.

He had never experienced anything like it. In those few stark, stunning split seconds it took him to connect with his wits, his shocked gaze had absorbed every long luscious inch of her, from her glossy black hair framing an exquisite heart-shaped face to the lush shape of her body enclosed inside a fitted jacket and a skirt that followed every long sinuous line of her curving hips, long slender thighs and shapely calves. And she was wearing boots, he noticed for some crazy reason. Little black leather ankle boots with heels like lethal spikes.

Then reality hit like a stinging shot of electricity to his wits and biting out a string of thick curses he slammed his foot down hard on the brakes.

Mia stood frozen as the low silver monster hurtled towards her, filling the air with a tire-burning, ear-piercing screech as the long silver bonnet came closer and closer until finally it slithered to a grit-spitting halt two tiny centimetres from her shins.

The engine hissed; the silver bonnet shuddered—silence returned like a numbing blow to the head. Pushing back into his seat, Nikos stared out at her with his heart pounding like a hammer and his fingers still clamped to the wheel. He had not believed he was going to stop in time. He wasn't even sure that he *had*. He continued to sit in a state of near-total shut-down, waiting for her to give him a clue by making some kind of movement—by stepping back to show he hadn't hit her or to drop down to the ground in a smashed heap!

Theos, she's beautiful, his stupefied brain fed to him, then compounded the observation by feeding a rush of hot blood down his front. It gathered in his loins like a neat shot of testosterone. Reacting to it with an explosive force of anger he thrust open the car door and threw himself out.

'What the hell do you think you are playing at!' he raked out in full blistering fury. 'Do you have a death wish or something? Why the hell didn't you move out of my way—?'

It took every bit of Mia's numbed strength just to breathe in and out. Her eyelashes finally gave a flutter of life and she managed to raise her eyes up from the car to focus on him instead. It came as a second shock to find she was staring at the most beautiful man she had ever seen in her life.

And he was striding towards her like a gladiator going to war. Only this gladiator had a black overcoat hanging from his impressive wide shoulders and wore a frighteningly elegant steel-grey three-piece suit beneath. His shirt was white, his tie a silky slither of smoke down his front.

Reaching the corner of the car he stopped to rake a downward glance at how close he had come to her fragile legs. Fire lit his eyes just before he reached out, clamped his hands around her waist and bodily plucked her off the ground. He was so intent on what he was doing he didn't seem to hear her sharp gasp of shock, or the heavy thud as her suitcase dropped from her taut fingers and hit the ground. The next thing Mia knew she was up close and staring directly into a pair of deep dark polished-mahogany eyes beneath startlingly straight thick eyebrows as black as the hair on his head.

'You stupid fool,' he roughed out, skin the same rich gold tones as ripening olives stripped so pale it accentuated his strong jaw set as hard as a clenched fist. 'Say something, for God's sake. Are you all right?'

Like a plastic doll jerked by hidden strings, Mia gave a shaky nod of her head. 'You—you almost killed me,' she whispered.

'I *avoided* trying to kill you,' he corrected. 'You should be thanking me for my fast reactions and skill.'

'You think it is skilful to drive like a lunatic, *signor*?'

'You think it is clever to stand stockstill in the middle of a private driveway while a car hurtles towards you, *signorina*?' he shot right back.

As if only just realising he had hold of her, he muttered something, then twisted around before dumping her back on solid ground away from the lethal bumper of his car. The sheer un-expectedness of the whole shocking incident jolted Mia's paralysed reflexes into action by forcing her to make a grab at his arms to steady herself when she almost toppled off the high heels of her boots. He braced his arms. Mia stared down at the amount of solid muscle and mighty male strength her fingers were clutch-ing at and snatched them away again.

Feeling her legs go strangely hollow she turned away from him, saw her suitcase lying like a battered victim on the ground a few feet away from them and went to straighten it up.

Pushing his hands into the pockets in his overcoat, Nikos watched her stoop to catch hold of the handle in her trembling fingers and could not stop his eyes from surveying the at-tractive shape of her derrière moulded to the fabric of her skirt.

Nice, he thought, then frowned darkly as another rush of heat shot down his front. Spin-ning away, Nikos took a frowning glance at his wristwatch. He was late, he saw. He had a plane to catch. He had just come away from one of the worst situations he had ever had to deal with, and he was standing around here admiring the rear view of the woman he'd almost just flattened into the ground with his car!

A sound of self-disgust escaped him. 'Try walking down the side of the drive from here,' he said loftily, then strode back the length of his car. 'And just for the record,' he added as he opened the door. 'If you're the new housekeeper they're all anxiously awaiting at the house, I think I should warn you you've gone over the top with the get-up.'

Straightening up from dusting off her suitcase, Mia blinked. Housekeeper... Get-up... Over the top...? She needed time to translate what he'd said so it would make some sense to her.

Then it did make sense. He thought she had come here to Balfour Manor dressed like this to take up the position of housekeeper.

Hurt gathered like a tight ball in her stomach. In all her life she had never felt hit so hard or so low. With the chilling cast of wounded dignity freezing her composure, she turned and walked herself and her suitcase around the bonnet of his fancy *over-the-top* supercar without bothering to offer him a single glance.

Housekeeper... Mia pushed out a strained

bitter laugh. She'd learnt to speak English while *housekeeping* for an ancient English professor who'd owned a villa not far from her home. He had paid her to keep his house clean and cook for him, and he had let her use his library and his computer so long as she typed up the pages of his endlessly long and boring tome. The English language course had been thrown in free of charge. Then she would walk the two kilometres back home and work on her school studies before spending the evening assisting Tia Giulia with the sewing she took in to help subsidise the meagre income *Tia* made growing cut flowers to sell in the nearest market town.

She usually wore sensible flat shoes and faded old jeans or one of the couple of dresses she had for the hot Tuscan summers. For the first time in her life she was wearing something new, not handmade out of a cheap bit of fabric she'd bought from a market stall. And that horrid man in his elegant silver car and his elegant silver suit and his elegant grooming which put him right at home here on the Balfour estate shattered her hard-worked-for self-confidence with just a few words.

Nikos narrowed his eyes as he watched her walk off down the driveway—hogging the middle of it like a defiance aimed exclusively at him. His lips gave a wry twitch. Instead of getting in his car and driving off, he stood and watched her for a few more seconds, drawn to do so by the graceful movement of her long curving figure, and her spark of spirit and the lingering echo of her throaty accent—Italian by the fire in it, he mused.

And young, he tagged on.

As in too young to be anyone's housekeeper?

The first seeds of doubt began to scratch at his conscience. Had he got it wrong and just insulted one of Oscar's daughter's friends?

Then it hit him what he was doing, and his frown came back as he climbed into his car and drove off down the drive. Whoever she was, he hoped she knew what she was walking into at Balfour Manor or she was in for one hell of a shock when she arrived.

Mia was already in shock because she'd just caught her first glimpse of Balfour Manor.

Nothing she'd read or seen on the Internet had prepared her for the sheer beauty of what she was looking at. Nestling in its own shallow valley, the stone-built house was at least ten times bigger than she had envisioned it to be, with row upon row of long casement windows glinting in the pale sunlight.

Trepidation began to fizz through the fine layers of her skin as she followed the driveway down into the valley and around the side of a pretty lake sheened like frosted glass. The closer she came to the house, the more intimidated she felt by it. It was huge. A grand stately home with tall palladium columns supporting a circular-shaped entrance, which dwarfed her courage along with her height as she walked between them and set her suitcase aside by a wall by the door.

Well, it was now or never, she told herself, and felt real trepidation clutch at her chest as she stepped in front of the heavy oak door.

Was she really certain she wanted to do this?

No, she wasn't any longer, but to turn away now, she knew she would regret it for the rest of her life because she would never find the courage to do this a second time.

On that stark piece of counselling, Mia reached out and gripped the old-fashioned bell pull and gave it a wary tug, her fingers lowering to her side again where they curled into her palms as she waited for someone to answer the door.

Nothing in her entire life had ever felt as frightening as this did.

Nothing had ever been as important to her as this.

Tense, trembling, eyes wide and wary as she watched the door start to open, the very last person she expected to see appear in its aperture was Oscar Balfour himself.

Taller and so much more dauntingly striking than she had envisaged him with his snow-white hair and neat goatee beard. When he frowned down he looked so terribly grim and austere she almost turned and ran. If he asked her if she was the new housekeeper she would run—she would, she decided.

But he didn't say it. He said, 'Hello, young lady,' and offered her a smile.

It was a nice smile, a kind smile which reached deep into the blue of his eyes.

Eyes the same colour blue as her own.

Eyes to which Mia clung. *'Bon...bon giorno, s-signor...'* Too nervous to stop herself from greeting him in Italian, she gulped and switched to stammering English. 'I don't know if y-you know about m-me but my name is Mia Bianchi? I have been told that you are my father...'

CHAPTER ONE

FOR the first time in three long hard-travelled months, Nikos Theakis strode in through the doors belonging to his London offices and instantly claimed the full attention of every person present in the slick modern granite-and-glass foyer.

Tall and dark, blessed with the kind of lean, hard, powerful body of a peak trained athlete, the air around him positively vibrated with excess energy as he moved, bringing forth a flurry of, 'Good morning, Nikos,' that sounded breathless and charged.

That he had the same effect everywhere he went said a lot about the man's personality. He was sharp, smooth, determined and driven. Working for him was like catching a ride on a rocket ship to the stars. Exciting, breathtaking, teeth-chatteringly scary sometimes because he took major risks others shied right away from.

He was committed and focused and famously never, ever wrong.

Today he was frowning, the two straight black bars of his eyebrows drawn together across the bridge of his arrogantly straight nose. The lean golden cut of his classical Greek features locked in concentration on the conversation he was involved in via his mobile telephone. His acknowledgement to the greetings therefore consisted of a series of distracted nods of his glossy dark head as his long stride took him across the foyer and into one of the waiting lifts.

'In the name of *Theos*, Oscar,' he swore softly, 'What kind of game are you trying to set me up with here?'

'No game,' Oscar Balfour insisted. 'I've thought this through carefully, now I am asking you for your support.'

'*Asking?*' Nikos pounced on the word with lethal satire.

'Unless you're too big and important now to help out an old friend…'

Stabbing a long finger at the top-floor button, Nikos shrugged back the brilliant white shirt cuff so he could check the time on his wafer-thin multifunction platinum watch, then bit back the desire to curse. He had been back in the country for less than an hour after spending weeks flying around the world like a damn satellite, putting together a rescue package for a crisis-embattled multiconglomerate which did not deserve to go under because its international investors had turned chicken and pulled the plug on their loans. He was tired, hungry and seriously jet-lagged but upstairs in his boardroom awaited a group of anxious people desperate to hear the final results of his toils.

'Stop trying to pull my strings,' he flicked out impatiently.

'I'm flattered that you think I still can,' Oscar drawled.

'And stick to the point,' he added, well aware that Oscar was the ruthless, cunning cut-throat king of manipulation so using that kind of invert flattery on him was wasted. 'Instead, tell me what in hell's name you expect me to do with one of your spoiled-to-death daughters?'

'Not bed her anyway.'

About to stride out of the lift into the hushed luxury of the top-floor corridor, that short cool evenly delivered statement froze Nikos to the spot for a second, the acid-bite affront hoisting up his proud dark head.

'That was not even remotely funny,' he denounced with icy cold dignity. 'I have never rested so much as a suggestive finger on any one of your daughters. It would be—'

'Disrespectful to me—?'

'Yes!' Nikos incised, for no one knew better than Nikos himself how much he owed to Oscar for turning him into the person he was today. Maintaining a respectful distance between himself and Oscar's beautiful daughters was a simple matter of paying honour to that debt.

'Thank you,' Oscar murmured.

'I don't want your thanks,' Nikos dismissed, and started moving again, covering the length of the corridor with the elegant grace of his long restless stride. 'And neither do I want one of your decorative daughters cluttering up my offices pretending to be a proficient PA just to please you,' he tagged on. 'Why this sudden decision to put them to work anyway?' he asked curiously as he pushed open the door to his own suite of offices.

His secretary, Fiona, glanced up from her computer screen and beamed him a welcome-back smile. Indicating to his mobile, Nikos gave a series of instructions via a long-fingered hand which the experienced Fiona showed she understood with a nod of her curly blonde head, leaving him free to shut himself inside his own office knowing the group of people waiting for him in the boardroom would be informed of his delay.

It was only as he shut the door behind him that he picked up the silence hanging heavy on the phone. It made him frown again because

Oscar Balfour possessed a brain which functioned at the speed of light so silences of any nature were unusual enough to cause Nikos a pang of concern.

'Are you all right, Oscar?' he questioned cautiously.

The older man released a sigh, 'Actually, I feel like hell,' he admitted. 'I have started to wonder what the past thirty years of my life have been about.'

Picturing this big tough larger-than-life investment tycoon with his snow-white hair and neat goatee beard and the pride of his long aristocratic heritage stamped onto every facet of him—

'You're missing Lillian,' Nikos murmured.

'Every minute of every hour of every day,' Oscar confirmed. 'I go to sleep thinking about her and spend the night dreaming about her, and I wake up in the morning searching for her warm body next to mine in the bed.'

'I'm—sorry.' It was a grossly inadequate response to offer, Nikos knew that, for Oscar Balfour was still grieving the recent loss of his wife. 'It's been a tough time for all of you...'

'With one death and two raging scandals following hard on the back of a world financial crisis which threatened to turn us all into beggars?' Oscar let out a dry laugh. '*Tough* doesn't cover it.'

Since Lillian Balfour's swift and untimely death three months ago, the great Balfour name had been rocked by scandal after scandal. From the moment Oscar took it upon himself to announce that he had a twenty-year-old daughter no one previously knew about, anyone with an axe to grind on a Balfour had come creeping out of the woodwork to air any grievance they might have. In short, Nikos mused, for the past few months the Balfours had been featuring in their very own no-holds-barred fly-on-the-wall documentary. It might not have been by consent but it had been scandalously spicy.

'You survived the crisis pretty well intact,' Nikos went for a positive note.

'So I did,' agreed Oscar. 'As you did.'

About to walk to his desk, Nikos found himself diverting across the room to go and stand in front of the large framed photograph of his home city he had mounted on the wall. If he narrowed his eyes he could just make out the murky dark spot down in the bottom corner, which represented the slum area of Athens where he'd spent the first twenty years of his life living by his wits from hand to mouth.

A nerve twitched along his hard jaw line, the rich colour of his eyes shadowing with his thoughts. Being street poor was as good an incentive he could come up with for working like a dog to ensure he would never be poor again, he pondered bleakly. And without the good fortune of an accidental meeting with Oscar, he would probably still be down there, living that same hand-to-mouth existence— with the odd spell in prison thrown in for good measure, he tagged on with a stark honesty that made him grimace.

This one man, this brilliant and shrewd, cunning-as-a-wily-fox Englishman had seen something in the arrogant young fool he had been back then, gone with his instincts and given him the chance to pull himself free of that life.

Made suddenly aware of the fine silk expense of his Italian suiting and his handmade shirt and shoes, Nikos turned to walk over to the plate of glass which gave his spacious top-floor office its famous London city views. He owned several other office buildings just like this one in the major capitals, along with the homes to complement his high-status lifestyle. He had the private yacht, the private plane, the personal investment portfolio to rival any out there…

The poor boy done good, Nikos quoted silently from a recent article an Athens newspaper had written about him.

Shame, he thought, about the scars he kept so deeply hidden inside even Oscar knew nothing about them.

'However, my daughters did not have a clue that there even was a world banking crisis,' Oscar's voice arrived in his ear once again. 'You're right, Nikos, I've spoiled them. I indulged their pampered princess lifestyles to a point of parental abandonment, and now I'm reaping the rewards for my neglect. I intend to put that right.'

'By cutting them off from your money and sending them out into the big bad world to sink or swim on their own—?' Despite the gravity in the conversation Nikos released a dry laugh. 'Trust me, Oscar, that's overkill.'

'Are you questioning my judgement?'

Yes, Nikos thought. 'No,' he deferred to the deep respect he held for this man, 'of course not.'

'Good,' Oscar said. 'Because I want you to take Mia under your wing and teach her everything she needs to know to survive as a Balfour.'

'Mia—?' Nikos repeated, needing a moment to connect with the unfamiliar name. 'Is she the—' He bit his teeth together, but too late.

'Is Mia—*what*?' Oscar demanded.

'The—new one,' Nikos described with what he thought was credible diplomacy considering the sensational way she had been outed as a Balfour.

'You can use the term illegitimate without offending me, Nikos,' drawled Oscar. 'Though I cannot be certain that Mia will feel the same way. She's—different than my other daughters… To put it bluntly,' Oscar sighed out, 'Mia just is not coping well as a Balfour. I think living in London and working alongside you will be good for her—teach her some self-confidence and toughen her up.'

'No way, my friend,' Nikos refused coolly.

'You can escort her to a few functions,' Oscar continued as if Nikos had not spoken. 'Show her how to play the social scene.'

'If she isn't coping within the safety of Balfour Manor, then what you're suggesting is the same thing as throwing her to the wolves,' Nikos pointed out. 'Take my advice and send her to one of the many matronly widows you know in London and let them teach her how to cope as a Balfour. I am a lone wolf, Oscar,' Nikos stressed. 'I always work alone and I *eat* the vulnerable.'

Another short silence sang down the phone line, only this one did not carry the heavy weight of grief like the last one had done. This one carried the stark chilling coldness of Oscar's sudden change of mood.

'I thought,' he said, 'we had already established that you don't *eat* my daughters.'

'I was not referring to—'

'Don't make me remind you that you owe me this, Nikos,' Oscar interrupted. 'Now I'm calling in the debt.'

Recognising the outright challenge which effectively pinned him to the floor with lead weights, Nikos tried for a last-ditch appeal. 'Oscar…'

'Are you going to refuse to do this favour for me?' Oscar cut in.

'No,' Nikos sighed out in heavy surrender. 'Of course I'm not refusing you.'

As Oscar had pointed out, he owed him—big time.

'Good. Then it's settled.' Oscar sounded warm again. 'And I thought that since you don't like live-in staff invading your private space, she could use the staff apartment attached to your London penthouse.'

Like a cornered animal Nikos thundered out, 'You mean you want me to *babysit* her as well as give her a job?'

'She will be with you tomorrow—be nice.'

Be nice, Nikos mocked as he tossed his mobile phone down on the top of his desk with more violence than the essential piece of equipment deserved, then turned to sink his lean hips onto the desk's polished edge.

In the act of honouring a moral debt he owed to Oscar, he had just agreed to compromise his own business values. A growl of bubbling frustration vibrated against his chest at the same moment a knock at his door heralded Fiona's appearance as she stepped into the room.

'Sorry to disturb you,' she murmured quickly, seeing the glowering frown pushing his flat black eyebrows together. 'But one of the Miss Balfours is down in reception asking to see you... She mentioned something about needing a spare set of keys to your apartment—?'

Nikos froze, as for the first time in his adult life he felt the rising tide of a hot blush try to destroy his legendary cool. What Fiona was really saying was that Oscar's new, shy, not-coping-very-well cuckoo had just strolled into his reception and made an announcement which effectively placed them in an intimate relationship!

She was not even supposed to arrive here until tomorrow. He had not even met her yet! Now the foolish woman had just set this whole damn building alive with hot and spicy speculation about the two of them!

Miss damn Balfour wasn't just foolish, she was outright dangerous!

Nikos leapt upright. To hell with being *nice*, he thought furiously as he strode right past the very curious Fiona and back down the corridor. In his experience you were not *nice* to a dangerous substance. What you did was treat it with cold hard respect while you carefully disposed of it.

Mia was standing by the reception desk already locked tautly into regret for blurting out what she had said in the *way* she had said it, when she saw the doors to one of the lifts slide open and a tall, dark, screamingly familiar man stride out.

Surprise closed her brain down for a second. She actually trembled on a moment of pure skin-tingling shock. His height, his colouring, his long hard body locked inside a crushingly elegant designer-cut business suit—it was the man who had almost run her over on the driveway of Balfour Manor on the day she had first arrived. Even the way he was coming towards her like a man on the war path screamed shocked recognition at her and filled her with the cowardly urge to start backing off.

'Oh, *Dio*,' she was unable to stop herself from gasping when he came to a stop an arm's length from her. 'It's you.'

His sentiments exactly, Nikos thought grimly. For he was suffering from the same stark shattering shock of recognition he could see written on her face, though he possessed the self-control to keep his shock under wraps.

Still, he did not seem able to prevent his eyes from making a thorough sweep of her tumbling-loose glossy-black hair and her simple white T-shirt with a short pale blue skirt. And she was wearing flat shoes, he noticed without wanting to. A pair of soft gold leather pumps which reduced her in height but did nothing to spoil the length of her fabulously long golden legs.

With barely a flicker of a silky black eyelash to say he'd understood what her shaken gasp represented, he questioned, 'Miss Balfour?' with clear cool polite formality. 'Since we have not met before, I am Nikos Theakis. It is a pleasure to meet you at last.'

He offered up a long-fingered hand for Mia to take. Skin-peelingly aware of the listening receptionist and all the other people in the foyer who were standing curiously about, Mia got the cold message his greeting conveyed to her and wanted to curl up and die where she stood. For someone who shied away from being placed in the spotlight, like a bat needed the cover of darkness just to live, she could not believe that she had made such a stupid error as to speak her reason for being here in a public domain like this.

Be brave had been the last words of encouragement her father had offered her just before his car had swept her away, she remembered. But being brave had absolutely nothing to do with what she was feeling right now as she forced her hand to lift up and settle warily against his.

'Bon—bon giorno,' she managed to respond while her eyes anxiously tried to convey an apology to him.

If he saw it he did not acknowledge it. If anything his lean hard-boned expression froze up all the more. 'I was not expecting you here until tomorrow,' he announced. 'However, I believe you have a domestic problem we need to sort out?'

'I… Yes,' Mia breathed in response.

Trying to ignore the sudden shot of electricity that stung through his palm when their hands touched, Nikos reclaimed his hand and took a quick glance at his watch. 'I have a meeting to attend,' he informed her briskly, 'but if you come with me, my secretary will deal with any problems you have.'

With that he turned and strode back across the foyer, with his thoroughly subdued new charge trailing in his wake. Throughout the whole thing he had not acknowledged the interested throng loitering in his foyer but his razor-sharp instincts were telling him he had successfully killed any juicy speculation as to why Mia Balfour was here.

Grimly pleased with himself for achieving that, at least, it was the only thing he was pleased about as he strode into the lift, then waited for her to join him.

'I am truly sorry!' she burst into anxious speech the moment the doors shut them in.

'You are a damn fool.' Nikos was not in the least bit impressed with her apology. 'If you're going to work with me, Miss Balfour, I suggest you learn the art of discretion quickly or you are not going to last a day.'

'I just did not think! Oscar told me to—'

'Let's leave your father out of this.' His dark eyes flashed her a look of contempt. 'When Oscar persuaded me to do this favour for him, I am convinced he would have established your agreement beforehand, which makes you responsible for your own actions, Miss Balfour. So, rule number one…you had better learn fast—don't ever embarrass me like that again.'

'I'm sorry,' Mia breathed for a second time, declining to try and add that it was Oscar who'd sent her here with the instruction to ask at reception for the keys to her new apartment. 'But a courier is due to arrive at your—m-my new address with my things and I n-need to be able to get in.'

'Try using a phone next time.'

Mia decided right there and then that she disliked Nikos Theakis.

'And to make a point, in case you have not yet realised it,' he continued with bite, 'you are here under sufferance. I don't work with fools. You will rise or fall on your own merits and if you don't pull your weight you're out. Got that?'

Beginning to feel just a bit annoyed now by his icy form of censure, Mia felt an unexpected urge to snap back at him. She had not deliberately set out to embarrass him after all. Why would she want to?

Tossing her head back, she looked at him standing there tall and erect with his contempt wafting over her in waves. He looked like what he was, a cold hard *angry* businessman, a thoroughly gorgeous, frighteningly successful *arrogant* Greek tycoon.

'And let's get one more thing straight before we leave this lift,' he went on. 'I am not into nepotism. I believe that everyone must work as hard as the next person to earn their place in the world.' One of the reasons Nikos knew he commanded so much respect from his employees was because he encouraged each one of them to explore their own potential no matter where they stood in the employment ranks. 'So you will pull your weight around here or you're out, got that?' he iced out.

'You think I am a useless freeloader,' Mia realised.

'Is a freeloader one step up from a house-keeper or one step down?' he threw back quick as a flash.

An angry flush bloomed in her cheeks. 'The housekeeper assumption was your mistake, not mine.'

'To which you took offence and flounced off like a fully fledged prima donna,' he threw back. 'I find it really curious to discover, three months later, that the day we met you were on your way to throw the whole Balfour family into a flat spin—as if they did not have enough to contend with at the time.'

Her moment of defiance crushed by that reminder, Mia pulled her guilty eyes away from his. He was referring to Oscar's poor wife, Lillian, Mia realised, and the way her unexpected arrival had caused so much trouble the after-effects were still rippling throughout the whole family today.

'I did not know that Lillian was ill,' she murmured defensively.

'But if *I* had known what you were up to that morning, I would have stopped you from going anywhere near them. Think about it,' he advised. 'If you'd lost the flounce and tried offering up an explanation to me, your arrival at Balfour Manor would not have been so badly timed because I could have stopped it from taking place, and the ensuing rush of shocks and scandals could possibly have been avoided.'

Could it really have been that simple? Mia wondered bleakly. Could a split-second decision made at a highly charged and very tense moment redirect the hand of fate as easily as that?

Ripples on a pond, she likened as the lift doors slid open and Nikos Theakis strode out, leaving her standing there feeling as if he'd just used her to wipe the floor with.

'I s-suppose you think it would have been better for everyone if you had just run me over.' She threaded after him.

Nikos paused five strides down the corridor, and turned around on the heels of his shoes. She was standing framed by the open lift doors with her hair flowing free around her shoulders and her beautiful face washed pale.

Young, he heard himself reiterate an observation he'd first made on the Balfour driveway. Guilty, vulnerable, hurt. In his anger he had just dumped full responsibility for the actions of the whole Balfour family upon her tense shoulders. Did he feel good about doing that?

No, he didn't. His punishment did not fit her crime.

And there was another element of this he had been trying hard not to focus on but he did so now by allowing his eyes to make a sweeping scan of her body and was instantly rewarded by a rush of heat down his front. It was the same rush of heat he'd experienced the first time he had seen her—the same one he'd been suffering every time he'd let his mind take him back to that moment on the Balfour's drive.

He was attracted to her. He'd been thinking about her on and off ever since. If he had been able to get back to the UK in the past months he would have been travelling down to Balfour Manor to try and find out who she was.

Now he knew.

She was a Balfour, which put her so out of bounds it effectively slammed shut the door to his attraction in his face.

So it went without saying that he did not want her invading his work place. He did not want her anywhere near him at all, threatening to mess up his nice calm business environment with her long lush figure and her soft sensual mouth and the promise of hot passion he could see gleaming behind the hurt blue of her eyes.

He took the cruel option and did not bother to answer her remark but instead turned away and strode on. He was behaving like a cold ruthless bastard and he knew it but it was the only way to protect himself.

He was about to give her one week—two, at most—before his cold hard critical assault on her vulnerable self-confidence sent her running back to Oscar in Buckinghamshire, Nikos told himself as he left Mia Balfour in the care of Fiona and went to chair his delayed meeting.

CHAPTER TWO

TWO long hard stubborn weeks later, Mia stood a good four paces back from the desk and sizzled inside with grim defiant patience while she waited for Nikos to acknowledge her presence.

She was wearing a simple-cut cream linen dress today, cinched in at her waist by a mustard-yellow leather belt, and on her feet she wore a pair of matching shoes. The whole outfit would have cost her full annual salary to buy new but as hand-me-downs went, Mia did not complain.

Would not dream of complaining. She was more horrified by the exorbitant price tags her half-sisters thought nothing of paying for the wear-once-and-discard clothes they crammed into the closets back at Balfour Manor. Hanging from a dress rail in the spare bedroom in her little apartment was a whole range of fabulous hand-me-downs just waiting for her eager fingers to unstitch and rework.

But *this* particular outfit had been picked off the rail with only one purpose in mind—to challenge Nikos Theakis to find anything objectionable about it.

He could frame a thousand criticisms with one sweeping glance from his cold dark eyes. And yesterday's objection had been aimed at the short pearl-grey skirt she had worn with a delicious plum-coloured silk georgette blouse. His sweeping glance of disapproval had taken in the length of leg she had on show and glittered with ice at the see-through fabric of the blouse even though she wore a matching camisole underneath it. So today she'd covered up in a dress with a hem that finished primly two inches below her knees. And she'd scraped back her hair into such a tight bun the skin framing her face felt tight, because yesterday he'd also snapped at her when she had to keep pushing the heavy weight of glossy black waves away from her face each time she'd looked down at her work.

And she was absolutely certain that he was deliberately making her wait like this to string out the tension by keeping his chair swung facing the window so all she could see of him was the top of his dark head.

It was all part of the war of attrition he was waging against her, because he hated having her working here as much as she hated having to *be* here. He was never going to forgive her for walking into a job she had not worked hard to earn, and she was not going to give up and run away from it because, for Oscar's sake and only Oscar's sake, she was determined to stick this thing out and learn to be the person her father wanted her to be even if it killed her in the process.

Or she killed Nikos Theakis.

Nikos was wondering if she had a single clue that he could read her thoughts through the back of his head. The trouble with Mia Balfour was that she was too young to have learnt the art of masking her feelings, and too *Italian* to want to do so if she could.

Murmuring a response to Petros, his Athens-based second in command, Nikos kept his brooding dark gaze fixed on the plate of tinted glass set between him and the view of London beyond, though he did not see the view. His attention was focused on the smoked glass itself, onto which Mia's image was stamped like a poorly exposed photograph, visible but misted by the daylight filtering in from outside.

There but not there, he likened. He preferred her like that, out of focus and out of reach so he could pretend that whatever else kept on charging up between them wasn't there either.

His call to Petros concluded, Nikos shut

down his mobile phone, took in a deep mental breath, then swung his chair around. An instant surge of testosterone-charged heat took a leap down his front to gather like a flaming knife in his groin.

The provocative witch, he thought, letting his eyes shutter out the telling gleam he felt spark to life in them while, at the same time, taking in every smooth sleek inch. The dress was a classy work of formal modesty, the pulled-back hair an insult to its fabulous long and waving length. Everything, even the length of her skirt, was telling him she'd corrected each criticism he'd aimed at her—spoken or unspoken.

His jaw line flexed. She missed damn well nothing.

Mia read the flexing tension as yet another display of criticism which threatened to crucify her self-confidence as much as it made her blood start to burn. She wished she could adopt the same physical indifference to him that he dealt out to her but she'd tried and she couldn't. Even though she hated him she could not stop herself from responding—inwardly, at least— to the pure male animal magnetism that poured out of him in such hot sinful waves. He made her feel breathless and snarled up by self-awareness she neither understood, nor could control.

'So, what have you got there for me?' he broke the silence, and even the rich deep tones of his voice made her insides quiver as she walked forward to place the file she was holding down on his desk.

'The information you wanted on Lassiter-Brunel,' she supplied.

Nikos glanced down at the bulky file, then back to Mia again, his lengthy black eyelashes flickering in surprise. 'That was quick.' Reaching forward he slid the file towards him. 'Did you stay up all night?'

'You said you wanted it by this morning,' Mia reminded him.

'So I did.' Lowering his gaze again, Nikos experienced a pang of guilt as he scanned through the sheets of information she'd compiled. He had a whole department of experts employed specifically to compile information like this which, he accepted uncomfortably, had made the work she had clearly put in here a complete waste of her time.

Then something unusual caught his attention. Sliding a slip of paper out from the rest he relaxed back in his chair to read.

Recognising what that something was made Mia tense, ready to be told that reading an old press piece she'd unearthed on the Internet describing Anton Brunel's less-than-nice reputation with the opposite sex was not what he expected to see in a business report.

One of his sleek black eyebrows rose upwards. 'You think this is appropriate information to include in here?' he made the predicted enquiry.

'It says he paid a lot of money to silence a female work colleague he had been—seeing.' Mia couldn't quite bring herself to say the descriptive words the article used.

'It *alleges* he paid hush money,' Nikos corrected.

'*Sí.*' Mia nodded to accept the correction. 'As you can see though, the lady in question filed sexual harassment charges which were then quickly dropped. If you look at the next document, you will find that on checking her out I discovered she had a child eight months later, a boy she named Anthony.'

'And your point?'

Mia tried not to pull in a deep breath. 'If a man is willing to abuse his position of power by seducing an employee, then pay her to keep silent about it, he is not reputable.'

'In your opinion,' Nikos pointed out.

'In my opinion,' Mia allowed.

'And if the—affair had been a mutual and amicable agreement, would that alter your opinion?' her interrogator enquired.

'He is married with children—'

'That was not my question.'

Mia shifted restively. 'The article says—'

'Alleges…'

'*Alleges,*' she echoed with the barest hint of a snap. 'She was quite distressed at the time she made the charges and she wore bruises on her arms and her face… There are photographs.' Mia pointed towards the file.

Allowing the lush curve of his eyelashes to droop again, Nikos looked at the photographs, the twist of his mouth showing his distaste before he used long fingers to slide the images aside.

'This article says that Brunel denied all knowledge as to how the lady acquired her bruises. He claims she set him up.'

'For what purpose would she do that?' Mia stared at him in bafflement.

'For the purpose of receiving the nice hefty pay-off she eventually got?'

'What about the baby?'

'Could be anyone's baby,' Nikos said with an indifferent shrug.

'But that is such a cynical way to view the situation,' Mia immediately flared up. 'You cannot know that for a fact, and—'

'You cannot know for a fact that Brunel's version isn't the truth,' Nikos cut in with incisive logic. 'I suspect the truth probably sits somewhere in the middle of both story versions, but since it was never proven either way I suppose we will never know.' Casting the sheet of paper aside he looked up at her. 'So tell me again why you included this in your report?'

Mia shifted from one foot to the other, not really wanting to answer that question. 'I—I don't like him,' she finally contrived to push out.

This time both sleek eyebrows rose upwards. 'But you've only met him once, the other day over lunch.'

'He has an—uncomfortable manner…'

Nikos suddenly lurched forward, his calm demeanour gone in a single sharp blink of his eyes. 'Explain that,' he commanded.

'I… No.' Feeling her cheeks start to heat, Mia lowered her gaze.

'You damn well will, Mia,' he countered harshly. 'And you will do it right now!'

'Why are you angry with me?' she queried hotly. 'You instructed me to find out everything I could about Lassiter-Brunel. I found these articles. You prefer that I pretended I did not?'

She was trying to divert the subject, Nikos recognised, narrowing his eyes as he swung his mind back to the working lunch they'd shared earlier this week with John Lassiter and Anton

Brunel. The two men were good-looking, arrogantly confident cut-throat businessmen—nothing wrong with any of those characteristics in people that strove for success.

However, his PA had been wearing a sexy red summer dress that fitted tightly beneath the voluptuous thrust of her breasts. The little black shrug thing she'd worn with it helped to cover nothing which mattered, and her hair had been drawn loosely back from her face in a big red clip. She'd looked like an exotic flower in a room packed with staid dark suits. Each time she let her big blue eyes drift across the lunch table the other two men lost the plot as to what they were talking about. Lush red lipstick, Nikos remembered. The warm and throaty tones of her Italian accent whenever she found the courage to speak.

Something he did not want to feel brought him to his feet with the smooth graceful movement of a leaping big cat. 'I want to know why you've decided you don't like Anton Brunel,' he insisted. 'Did he say something to offend you?' he quizzed sharply. 'Did he make a pass?'

Wishing now that she had not started this by including that article, Mia shifted uncomfortably. 'No—'

'What then—?' he shot at her.

'It was n-nothing!' Her eyes widened in

alarm when he came striding around the side of the desk and pulled to a stop only when he towered right over her. Intimidated by the whole macho physicality of his stance, Mia took a wary step back. 'W-what is the matter with you?' she husked out.

'Just answer the question.' Nikos stepped in close again, halting her next backward step by catching hold of her arms to make her stay where she was.

Feeling the pressure of his fingers slither a streak of heat over her shoulders, Mia hurriedly tried to bury the sensation in a rush of speech. 'He—he said something I took offence to when—when we were leaving and you were talking to John Lassiter.'

'What did he say? And look at me when you talk to me,' Nikos rasped in annoyance. 'It infuriates me when you hide your eyes from me like that.'

Pulling in a tense breath, Mia did as he bade her, found herself clashing with a pair of polished-mahogany eyes, a flame in their depths she had never seen there before. For a second she forgot what they were talking about while she absorbed this fascinating new discovery and—

'Speak,' Nikos commanded.

Mia blinked, elaborately long soot-black eyelashes a trembling framework around the startling rich blue of her eyes. 'He—he claimed I was m-making the big eyes at him, then made a—a personal remark about you and me,' she enlightened. 'It's your own fault, Nikos!' she then flared up before he could react. 'You make me follow you about like a pet dog on a leash! You glare at me if I move. You glare at me if I smile. You touch my hair, my arm, my fingers if I rest them on the table. You slide your hand around my waist when we walk! Look at you now,' Mia charged up heatedly. 'You are holding me here in front of you as if you have some special right to do so! That horrible man must have misread the signals you were giving, and dared to tell me he would like to enjoy a little slice of what y-you were getting from me!'

Nikos snapped his fingers from her arms as if she'd burned him. Mia almost staggered off the heels of her shoes in shock. The stunned expression on his face made her wring out a little laugh. 'You don't know you do it, do you?' she choked out unsteadily. 'You have no clue at all that you do any of the things I said! Well, you do, and he assumed from *your* behaviour towards me that we are—intimate.' The word struggled to leave her throat. 'And—and he asked me if I would like to meet with him one afternoon when you were unavailable.'

Nikos turned to stone in front of her. Shaken up by what she had just said to him, Mia tried to tug in a strained breath. In the two weeks she'd been working with him, Nikos had been treating her more like his lowly slave than his personal assistant. He'd dragged her out to every business luncheon he had attended. He'd brought her tumbling out of bed at ungodly hours of the morning to accompany him to working breakfasts too. If she spoke he didn't like it; if she smiled he didn't like it. If she let her attention drift to take in her surroundings he touched her hand to bring her gaze back to him, then frowned at her as if she had committed a mortal sin. Then he dumped her back at her apartment in the evenings and left her there alone—to recover, she presumed, while he went out and—did whatever it was he did in the evenings with whoever it was he did it with!

'So we drop the Lassiter-Brunel deal.'

Tuning in too late to catch what he'd said, Mia saw that he'd moved back round his desk and lowered himself back into his chair again.

'See to it,' he instructed, pushing the now-closed folder back across the desk.

'S-see to wh-what?' she stammered out warily.

He lifted eyes to look at her. It was like being pinned to the wall by shards of black glass. Whatever it was that had exploded inside of him was gone now and the cold hard ruthlessly controlled animal was back.

'I'm s-sorry,' she felt compelled to apologise. 'But I did not catch w-what you s-said to me.'

'My command of the English language is that poor?' he mocked.

'N-no.' She *hated* him. 'I l-lost concentration f-for a m-moment...'

Nikos wondered what she'd do if he asked her to use that delightfully husky stammer she'd just developed, tonight while lying naked beneath him in his bed?

Theos! The silent curse burned its way around his head in protest for letting his imagination go in that direction. Two damn long weeks of this and she was still here driving him crazy.

Did he really do all of those things she had listed or was she just out to pull his strings—?

A curse locked in his throat. His new PA might not like him, but she lusted after him with a fever she was too inept to keep hidden, though he was equally certain that she was not aware that she was so transparent.

And *that* was the reason Anton Brunel had picked up on the sexual vibrations at the lunch table, he determined. Her fault, not his fault. And as for all that touching stuff she'd accused him of—it only happened inside her overimaginative head.

She made him think of a living, breathing sexual grenade with the pin dangling halfway out—half precocious woman, half infuriating child—and she might heat him up like no women had ever done, but he did not want her in his bed!

Oscar would never forgive him.

On that final sense-cooling reminder, Nikos made a grab at the thread of this discussion. 'Call John Lassiter,' he instructed. 'Tell him I'm no longer interested in doing business with them.'

'Me—?' Mia gasped. 'But I don't want—'

'And bring me some coffee,' he cut over her scared protest and sat forward to pick up his pen.

If this didn't teach her to keep her provocative ways in check, then nothing would. The Lassiter-Brunel deal was worth several million on paper. The innately frugal Mia Bianchi-Balfour was going to gag at the loss of such a lucrative deal. 'And remind Fiona I will be out for two hours at lunch.'

'But...Nikos *please*,' Mia murmured painfully. 'I don't know how to do what you said!'

'Make coffee?' he incised with a cruelty he actually enjoyed inflicting.

'Tell somebody a deal is to be broken!'

'Then you are about to ride yet another steep learning curve,' he relayed without a hint of care. 'And just for the record, I don't approve of office affairs, romances or even friendships. So stop taking swipes at me by the way you dress, or the way you look at me, or the way you put that Lassiter-Brunel file in front of me, expecting me to find that article and question your motives so you could tell me what Brunel presumed about us. It was irritating and juvenile. There is no *us*. The rest of what you said lives only in your head. Now I have some calls to make.'

Dismissed, appalled, devastated—*whipped* by his cold assassination—Mia spun away and walked across his office on legs that shook.

Irritating and juvenile....

'I hate him,' Mia whispered once she was on the other side of the door.

'Did you say something?' Fiona glanced up from her work.

Wishing she was dead or at least far, far away from this place, Mia stumbled across the room to sink down in the chair behind her desk before her trembling legs crumbled altogether. 'He's in a very bad mood today and I hate him.'

'Don't we all, darlin',' Fiona responded dryly. 'Our gorgeous boss is pure sex on legs but as cold as ice. It's such a waste of good male flesh.' Sitting back from her computer console, Fiona's floppy blonde curls bounced on her head as she gave Mia's pale face the once-over. 'Bit your head off, did he?'

More than just my head, Mia thought tragically. 'I don't know how you have put up with him for as long as you have.'

'I'm immune.' Fiona waggled her left hand at Mia, showing off the three sparkling rings she wore on her marriage finger. 'I've got my own sexy brute to go home to each evening, and he's never cold.'

'He wants me to cancel the Lassiter-Brunel deal.'

Fiona went still. 'So you told him.'

Mia pressed her trembling lips together and nodded. 'He didn't believe me.'

'Then why is he pulling out of the deal?' the secretary quizzed with a frown.

'To—to punish me,' Mia answered. 'He knows I don't know how to do such a thing so he's making me do it to teach me a lesson about the consequences of making up stories.'

'Nikos Theakis is throwing away a lucrative deal just to teach you a lesson?' Fiona laughed. 'I don't believe it. There has to be more to his reasoning than that.'

There was, Mia thought bleakly. She had told

him some other things he had not wanted to hear about. 'And he's not taking me with him to his lunch today…'

And that harsh rebuff was striking her as hard as everything else. It was like being cut off from the main lifeline which kept her functioning. She might hate him but she revelled in being around him.

Why had she told him he constantly touched her? Why hadn't she kept her big mouth shut?

'Perhaps that's a good thing,' Fiona said gently.

Blinking her ridiculously long eyelashes Mia brought her gaze into focus on the other woman, read her sympathetic expression and went hot.

'He wants coffee.' Looking away she stood and walked across the office to the coffee machine to prepare a small tray, then on impulse she begged Fiona, 'Will you take it in? I don't think I can stand another visit in there right now.'

'Sure…' Always relaxed, always sunny, Fiona came to take the tray from her, then paused. 'Mia…' she posed gently, 'take a bit of advice from someone older and wiser than you are…get yourself a man.'

Glancing up, she groaned, 'Oh, *Dio*. Am I so obvious?'

Fiona's sympathetic smile said it all. 'You know, when you first arrived here everyone in the building was more than ready to dislike you for who you are and how you came by this job. It took you just a week to win us all over. You're hard-working, sweet and nice, but he isn't nice—to women.'

Mia started despising herself for bringing this lecture on.

'He uses them, Mia,' Fiona pressed on her. 'He does not respect them.'

'As they use him.' She felt some crazy need to defend Nikos Theakis even though he did not deserve it.

'Yes.' Fiona couldn't argue with that. 'Especially Miss Supermodel Lucy Clayton who received her farewell gift by special messenger last week. By next week another woman just like her will have been put in her place. It's the way he works. The way he likes to keep it,' Fiona stressed. 'He's an amazing risk taker in the business arena. An absolute financial genius everybody admires and respects, and he's commendably honest and committed to any promises he makes—in business—but in his personal life?' Fiona shook her head. 'He's a smooth, cool, bone-meltingly gorgeous sexual predator. He does not connect sex with his emotions—if he has any—the jury is still out on that. So take my advice and don't go there. Don't even *want* to go there because if he decides to take you he will spoil you for ever. So get yourself a man,' she repeated, 'and wean yourself off him while you still can.'

'Where is my coffee?' the sexual predator demanded.

CHAPTER THREE

BOTH women jumped guiltily and turned to see Nikos Theakis standing in his office doorway. By his closed expression there was no way they could tell if he'd overheard them talking about him, but for the first time since she'd started working here, Mia saw two hot coins of guilt hit Fiona's creamy cheekbones and knew her own cheeks wore the same hot sting.

Good, Nikos thought, tamping down hard on his anger for the second time this morning as he strode across the room to take the tray from his blushing secretary, then strode back into his office with it without uttering another word.

Get yourself a man... His lips compressed into a tight line as he set down the tray. Why had he not thought of offering his PA the same piece of advice?

The answer to that question was not a nice one. But then, as his secretary had just pointed out to Mia, he wasn't *nice*.

It rankled—the not-nice part and the man part.

Throwing himself down in his chair Nikos swung it around to face the window. *So I don't respect women.* A flash of irritation shot across his face. He *did* respect them or why the hell did he restrict himself to the kind that preferred to play the game the way he liked to play it? He wasn't looking for love. He was not looking for marriage, so he steered well clear of the kind of women looking for either or both.

And that was respecting them, he determined. It would have been *nice* if Fiona had recognised that.

Vaguely surprised that there was a dose of hurt rolling round inside him, Nikos frowned. He was good to his staff, fair—generous, as Fiona had pointed out. He'd believed he had their *respect*. His secretary had shocked him with her view of him. It angered him that she'd felt it necessary to warn Mia off.

He rested a long forefinger along the line of his mouth where the smooth skin covering his lips felt tightly stretched, his eyes narrowed by an unwanted feeling of distaste at the idea of Mia turning all of that untapped passion on for some other man.

What if she took Fiona's advice—?

'Damn,' he muttered, not liking what was rattling around inside him. Where was the guy who focused purely on business? The guy who barely noticed a woman unless she was stretched out naked on a bed?

Perhaps that was it. He needed a woman. *Sex*, he named it. A long night of seething hot passion with the kind of woman who could appreciate what he could do for her without expecting the whole heavy emotional bit by return. He was not possessive. He was not even mildly demonstrative like Mia had dared to suggest. If he touched her like she said he did, it was done with attention to polite good manners and *respect*. She was the one who'd misread the signals.

John Lassiter was at first stunned by Nikos Theakis's decision to pull out of negotiations, then he grew increasingly more angry by Mia's apologetic inability to give him answers as to why they were being dumped. Within minutes of her finally managing to put the phone down on the uncomfortable conversation, Fiona's telephone was ringing and Anton Brunel was demanding to speak to Nikos.

With a telling glance at each other, Fiona put the call through to their boss. Ten minutes later he was striding out of his office with his too-handsome face locked into an iron-hard mask of contempt. He did not speak as he crossed their office; he did not cast them a glance. The dismissive tension he left behind him cloyed on Mia.

In the end, she couldn't stand it, and she took herself off to the café around the corner to buy herself some lunch. While she sat at one of the small tables trying to eat a sandwich her tense throat did not want to swallow, a man from the accounts department came in to the café. Seeing her sitting on her own he brought his sandwich to her table and joined her.

After a shy start to her unexpected company Mia surprised herself by warming to his easy-going brand of friendly humour and began to relax and enjoy herself. They walked back to the office building together and lingered to finish their conversation in the foyer for a minute or two. It was all warm and nice and friendly and fun.

Striding into his plush grey-and-black marble foyer, Nikos caught sight of his PA standing there, talking with someone from his accounts team.

Shock almost brought him to a halt.

She looked young and beautiful and relaxed and alive. Something hard and hot grabbed hold of his chest and hung on. Without knowing he was about to do it, he parted his grim lips to snap out her name, only to clamp them shut again when her 'pet dog on a leash' accusation leapt into his head.

He kept himself moving towards the bank of lifts and refused to look at the cosy duo again. Once he'd gained the privacy of his luxurious office, he went straight on the offensive and took out his mobile phone to start flicking through his address book. Five minutes later he had arranged dinner for that evening with the beautiful and very eager Lois Mansell and was feeling much better about himself. Lois was just what he needed. She was a cool smooth banking executive practiced in the art of sex just for sex. Young and irritatingly naive brunettes with more than a hint of Italian fire in their bellies, and with *virgin territory* stamped all over them, did not and never would do it for him.

Get yourself a man... Mia considered this as she sat alone in her flat that same evening, reworking a designer suit to look less high fashion and more office friendly so she could wear it to work next week.

Weaning herself off Nikos Theakis was making good sense the more she thought about it. He did not want her. *Dio*, he had gone into great detail to make it clear how much he did not want her!

Irritating and juvenile...

Putting her sewing aside she stood with a

tense jerk and paced restlessly over to the window to look out. It was dark outside, the London night skyline twinkling with lights. It was Friday night and most people of her age would be out there enjoying themselves, but here was she alone in her flat with her hair stuck in a ponytail, wearing a pair of faded jeans and an old top, and no plans to go anywhere, or anyone to call upon if she did want to go out!

Right now she would kill to have a man ring her doorbell, or to be getting ready to go out to meet with him.

Fiona was right. It was time she weaned herself off this infatuation she suffered for Nikos Theakis. It was time for her to throw off the shy little country girl and make good use of the opportunity her father had given her to grow into herself.

A man…a man… How did one go about attracting a man?

Well, not by standing alone here in her flat, that was certain. Could she have enticed the man she'd shared lunch with today to ask her out, if she'd put her mind to it?

Her isolated life in Tuscany had not taught her anything about being a young independent woman living on her own in a big city. She'd lived all of her life with her aunt on a small hill farm five kilometres from the nearest village.

She'd attended a tiny convent school for girls, and money had been so tight that even meeting her school friends in the nearest town on a Saturday to go shopping together had been beyond her meagre cash reserves.

In her life to date, she'd had just two abiding influences. A wonderfully caring but ageing aunt she adored, and an even older man she kept house and cooked for who lived very much in a world of his own. And the worst part was that no matter how hard Oscar and his daughters had tried to bring her out of herself, she was still that quiet, shy and isolated country girl on the inside.

She sighed, turning to face the room again with its bland walls and bland modern furniture and its television playing softly in the corner for company.

I'm going to go out.

The decision sparked out of nothing. It just hit her like a fever in her head and, before she knew it, Mia was striding out of the sitting room and into the bedroom. Ten minutes later she returned, dressed in a short dusky-lilac silk dress with a dipping neckline and tiny lace-cap sleeves. A hunt along the rail of hand-me-downs had uncovered a fashionably complicated fitted black satin jacket she pulled on over the dress as she walked.

And most important of all, her resolve to just get out there and *do* something was burning like a fire in her blood. Gathering up her purse she let herself out of her flat and crossed the plush creamy oval-shaped foyer to press the button to call the lift up to the top floor.

She was going to find a restaurant and eat out for a change. Lots of cool independent people in London dined alone. She'd seen them doing it at the lunches Nikos had taken her to so why not go and do it herself?

Brave Mia, she mocked, feeling tense tingles play havoc with her insides in direct opposition to the adventure she was about to embark upon. Because she wasn't brave. Never had been. And if the lift didn't arrive soon she was going to—

The sound of a door opening behind her had her spinning about. Instantly her tingling insides crashed to a fizzing burn when she found herself staring at Nikos.

It just was not fair that he had to pick this moment to leave his apartment, she decided as she stared at him in dismayed shock.

He was wearing a formal black dinner suit that sat smoothly on his long powerful frame. A black silk bow tie sat perfectly symmetrical across the butterfly collar of his dress shirt. And his hair was still damp, as if he'd dressed quickly after showering now the hint of curls lay black and thick and glossy on the top of his well-shaped head. Every single inch of him looked strong and sleek and formidably exclusive. Her mouth ran dry and her heart started beating too fast as she flickered her gaze up to stare at his recently shaved jaw, then the sensual shape of his unsmiling mouth. And finally— finally she made contact with his eyes.

He was looking back at her as if this accidental meeting had disconcerted him as much as it had done to her. Defensive tension stiffened her stance.

'On your way out?' he spoke first, smooth and cool and, Mia suspected, carefully pleasant.

'*Sí*,' she managed, unaware that her hands had clenched into fists on the ends of her arms held straight like sticks at her sides.

He nodded, the floating veil of his eyelashes sweeping downwards before he turned to pull the door to his apartment shut.

Fortunately the lift arrived then, giving Mia a good reason to drag her eyes away from him, though it made little difference, she realised a few seconds later, when the lift's mirrored walls allowed her to watch him stride across the lobby and join her inside. The small space instantly grew even smaller, crammed by his superior height and that overpowering sense of presence he always carried around with him.

But then, the mirrors were giving her two or three or even four different views of him. That was a lot of Nikos Theakis to contend with in a confined space. Her breath caught again when he leant across her to hit the button to take them down to the ground floor. The subtle tangy scent of him assailed her nostrils. As his sleeve brushed against her arm she took a step back. So did he, straightening to his full formidable height.

'Anywhere nice?' he enquired casually.

Keeping her eyes glued to her own reflection, Mia nodded and watched her hair move against the black satin jacket. 'Dinner,' she said, watching her lightly glossed lips part to form the response.

When she looked into her eyes she had no choice but to acknowledge the lurking darkness of deep uncertainty at her impulsive decision to go out like this. Was she mad? Was she stupid? What did she know about surviving in this huge metropolis? She didn't even know whether to turn to the left or to the right when she reached the street. The left led downtown where the more refined restaurants were situated. The right led to the local high street with its trendy bistros and café bars she passed on the occasions she caught the tube home and walked the rest of the way back here.

Left or right? Refined or trendy?

'You?' she asked because she felt she should do.

'Same.'

She looked up—not wanting to—and wished she had not when she found him checking out the set of his black bow tie in one of the mirrors, chin thrust upwards, beautifully black-framed eyes as dark as night. Sensation sprinkled like static between fine layers of her skin and she looked away again quickly, back to the stranger she saw herself as, dressed in a dusky-lilac shift dress and a black satin jacket, with a lot of long leg showing and her ankles elevated by the four-inch heels on her shoes.

Irritating and juvenile…

Was he on his way to meet the new replacement for Lucy Clayton as Fiona had predicted? Was she tall and blonde and heart-stoppingly beautiful and screamingly intelligent and sophisticated? Was he planning to bring her back here to his apartment to make wildly passionate love with her while Mia lay alone in her bed next door and—

'Where—?'

Her small chin jerked up and their eyes clashed in a mirror; tiny prickles of attraction attacked her flesh. *'Scusi?'* she murmured blankly.

'I was asking where you are going for dinner,' Nikos enlightened dryly—in English.

'Oh. I don't know,' Mia let slip before she could think about it, watched his eyebrows arch, felt a deep inner niggle at the slip, then thankfully her pride came to her rescue with what she thought was a truly inspirational lie. 'I am meeting someone,' she claimed. 'I don't know where he is taking me to eat.'

Fortunately the lift stopped and the doors slid open then, giving her the opportunity to escape. Her shiny black heels tapped on cream marble as she crossed the ground-floor lobby in her urgency to get away as fast as she could.

Nikos still reached the door in time to open it for her, then offered a cool nod in acknowledgement of her muffled murmur of thanks.

It must have been raining. Outside the ground was covered in a shiny layer of wet. Striding out across the private car park, Mia was aware that he had diverted over to where his silver car was parked.

What she did not know was the way Nikos stood watching her pause uncertainly once she'd hit the street, as if she was unsure which way to go next.

Dinner with a man...

Something hard gave him a kick in his gut.

Was she meeting the tall blond clean-cut guy from accounts he had seen her with today?

If she was, the damn jerk needed to learn some manners. What kind of man let a young and beautiful stranger to this city find her own way to their chosen venue?

She looked lost already. And the weirdest kind of tingling sensation was skittering down his torso and legs.

She struck off to the right, disappearing out of his sight in seconds. Nikos held his stance for a few seconds longer, then he muttered, 'Damn it,' giving in to what the tingling represented and slid his hand into his pocket to exchange his car keys for his mobile phone.

Ten minutes later, Mia was hovering outside one of the bistros. She was pretending to read the menu list stuck on the window but really she was checking out the busy interior, and the bravado that had brought her this far was now lying dead at her feet.

She could not go in there. She did not know why she had ever come up with the crazy idea that she could! And the evening was chilly, the black satin jacket doing nothing to keep the chill at bay and—

'Been stood up…?'

Hearing that deeply accented, mildly sardonic and crushingly familiar voice arrive from somewhere behind her caused a sudden burn of weak tears to flood her eyes. It took every bit of self-control she had to blink the tears away again, then lift up her chin and turn to look at him.

He was standing across the busy pavement, leaning against the side of his silver supercar with his hands resting inside his trouser pockets, his jacket pushed back from his bright white shirt. Tall, dark and so very sexily sophisticated, Mia observed helplessly. The overhead lights shining amber onto the wet pavement also honeyed the skin of his too-perfect face. It was no wonder most of the women passing across the gap between them stared at him, Mia thought as a whole clutch of them went by with their eyes glued to his long, lean, supremely elegant stance.

If he noticed he did not show it. He did not take his eyes from her face. His mouth was wearing a kind of half-mocking smile that stung her pride and made her wish that some other tall, dark, handsome man would just walk up to her and pull her into his embrace.

Irritating and juvenile...

'No,' she answered his question. 'He's just a few minutes late.'

With the ease of a man used to doing everything with grace, she watched him tilt his dark head down and, without removing his hand from his pocket, twist his wrist, shrug back his shirt cuff and somehow manage to display his watch.

'This is not the kind of place a man keeps a woman waiting out on the pavement, *cara*,' he said when he looked back at her again.

'Well, you should know since you seem to be doing the same thing to your date,' Mia fired back.

'I pick my dates up at their door.'

'Then please go and do so,' she invited and turned back to the bistro window.

The seconds ticked by. Her ears pricked and her senses went on the alert for the sound of his car driving away. She found the space around her suddenly swamped by a group of people who wanted to check out the menu too. By the time they'd moved on she was wishing she'd had the foresight to tag on to them.

Because he was still there. She could feel his silent presence like some dark force trying to drag her back round to face him. After another second or two she heard him sigh, then the sound of his footsteps bringing him close. Tension zinged down her backbone and remained there stinging like an electric charge. A second later he was standing right behind her—she could feel his body heat along her back.

'Will you go away,' she snapped. 'You are making me feel stupid!'

'Once your date arrives,' he agreed. 'Who is he anyway?'

Keeping her eyes fixed rigidly on the bistro window, she said, 'That is none of your business.'

'No?' A hand moved against her spine like a finely brushed admonishment. 'I'm the guy who's been placed in charge of your care, so that makes it my business.'

'I do not need a babysitter.'

'Nor do you need a man who plans to sit you down to dine in a place like this. It's a bog standard pizza place, Mia, with a cheap and fast turnaround.'

Was it—? Mia stared at the menu, still none the wiser having never eaten at such an establishment. Until Nikos had taken her with him to his working lunches she had never eaten in a restaurant at all!

'You will be outside again before you know you've eaten,' he predicted. 'What happens, then? An hour or so in one of the pubs dotted down the street to soften you up with a couple of glasses of cheap wine, or will he be expecting to go straight back to your place to finish off the evening in the comfort of your bed?'

'Well, you should know since you are fabled for your fast turnaround,' she swung round to fling at him and was very pleased to see that likening his dating skills to a fast pizza restaurant made his chiselled jaw clench.

'That was not what I—'

'*Grazie*, for your wise advice,' Mia cut him off midsentence. 'When my date arrives I will be certain to ask him what his intentions are.'

'Or I will.'

Sparking up like a firework she gasped out, 'No you will not!'

'And he's not only unforgivably late he's unfit to date a Balfour.'

Half unwilling to believe they were even having this conversation, Mia stared up at him. 'And you believe you have the right to make that judgement?'

'In your father's place—yes.'

In other words she was a *duty* he felt compelled to oversee! 'Well, you are not my father—or my idea of what a father figure should be! And in case you have forgotten,' she added stiffly. 'You went out of your way to tell me to back off from irritating you, so now I am telling you to do the same thing for me, Nikos, and just go away!'

With that she turned to walk off down the high street. His long fingers curling around one of her shoulders held her still.

'Mia, this is stupid,' he sighed out heavily.

Or irritating and juvenile... Why was that cutting remark still stinging her as badly as this? Mia asked herself.

She did not know. She did not understand what she was feeling or even what she was *doing* any more.

'Please let go of me...' She tried to move away from him.

His fingers tightened gently. 'No,' he refused. 'Look...' he said, 'I'm—sorry if I sounded... insensitive to your feelings but—'

'Sounded it?' she threw out.

'*Was* insensitive, then,' he altered, the chiselled line of his jaw clenching. 'But it does not change the fact that your so-called date has either stood you up or is only too happy to leave you to stand around here like a fool!'

'And that is your sensitive side talking?' So close to tears now, she had to push a hand up between them so she could cover her trembling mouth.

A soft curse rattled from him. '*I* will take you to dinner,' he offered, sounding so driven to say it that Mia almost snapped the hand up higher to slap his face!

But she didn't because it would be *irritating and juvenile* of her to do it! 'I can provide my own dinner,' she told him stiffly. 'And you already have a date.'

'I did have a date until—' Nikos stopped, compressing his lips, then dealt her a glinting glimmer of a look '—until I was stood up too,' he finished dryly.

'You—?' It was like discovering he had a chink in his impenetrable armour. Mia was so intrigued by the phenomenon she stopped fighting his grip to stare up at him instead.

'It happens to the best of us,' Nikos compounded on his quick-thinking masterpiece of deception. 'So shall we find somewhere quieter than this to—commiserate with each other while we eat?'

Like a lamb to the slaughter, he mocked, feeling his conscience pinch him when his beautiful PA dealt him a sympathetic look.

But at least the deal was done.

CHAPTER FOUR

TWENTY minutes later they were being shown to a table in a very exclusive restaurant and the waiter was taking away her jacket while Mia glanced around.

If this was the kind of place Nikos tended to frequent, then she was willing to be impressed by its softly lit ambience.

'Have I been here before?' she asked.

'Not to my knowledge.'

Surprising him with a sudden grin she told him, 'If you have not brought me here for one of your business lunches, Nikos, then I have not been here. These kinds of places all have a similar look to them, don't they?'

'Do they?' He glanced around their plush, hushed award-winning surroundings. 'Perhaps you're right.'

Mia nodded. 'They probably look different in the daylight when they are filled with sharp-suited men and women looking serious and intelligent instead of…' Her voice trailed off, even white teeth pressing down into her lower lip to halt the potentially provocative word she had been going to use.

'Intimate.' Nikos was not so sensitive. 'It's called good business sense,' he enlightened. 'Not the people but the restaurants,' he explained what he'd meant. 'They change their mood with the mood of the city. By day they provide the sharp suits like me with a place to work while we eat.' A dryness entered his voice. 'By night they soften their appearance to provide a more relaxed ambience for their more sociable clientele. I love the dress…'

'Oh.' Startled by the sudden and totally unexpected compliment Mia blushed as she glanced down at the lilac silk dress. 'It used to belong to my sister Bella.' Critical fingers plucked at the dress's dipping cleavage. 'There used to be a strip of lace here but I unpicked it because I thought it looked less fussy without it.'

'Oscar has not provided you with your own wardrobe?'

His eyes were slow to rise to catch her brief shrug. 'He offered. But I did not see the need to buy more new clothes when the closets at Balfour were stuffed full of things no one else wanted to wear.'

A young waiter arrived to offer them menus then. Mia winged him a warm smile and when she realised he was Italian she fell into conversation with him. Veiling his eyes Nikos observed the change in her as she talked. Her voice had taken on a warm and earthy vibrancy Nikos had not heard before. The young waiter fell in love with her as Nikos watched. She had no idea of the power she was wielding, had not even noticed the waiter's darkened eyes and the raised colour in his face. When her slender hands joined in the conversation the waiter was hooked, his eyes fixed on the creamy cleavage on show behind the expressive fingers.

And Nikos felt a sudden blistering urge to punch the young fool! Perhaps he moved, he wasn't sure, but something made the waiter glance his way. The next second he was rushing out an apology and moving away at lightning speed.

'He comes from San Marcello,' Mia enlightened him as if his Italian was not good enough to follow their conversation, and with no clue at all what had made the waiter take flight as if someone had set fire to his heels.

Nikos knew. He could still feel the trails of it lingering behind his veiling eyelids. 'A neighbour, then,' he murmured.

'*Sí*, by a hilltop or two.' Settling back into her

seat she shook the silky fall of her hair back from her face, then picked up her menu.

When he continued to sit there doing and saying nothing she glanced up at him and frowned, then followed it up with a sigh. 'OK, what have I done to annoy you this time?' she demanded. 'Have I broken some very important rule of dining that is likely to earn me a plate of cold food?'

'Brunel would call it breaking the rules anyway,' he responded impassively.

'Brunel…? What has he got to do with…'

Enlightenment dawned. Mia flicked a look across the restaurant to where the friendly waiter now stood to attention, striving to keep his eyes away from this corner of the room.

'You are accusing me of flirting,' she said in a hushed breath of stunned disbelief.

Nikos picked up his menu and opened it. 'You tied him in knots. For a few interesting seconds I thought he was going to pull out a chair and join us.'

'We were just *talking* about *Italy*!' Mia impressed upon him in self-defence.

'I got this really bad feeling that I was about to be sidelined. Not good for my ego at all.' Nikos smiled. 'Lesson one in the use of social skills, *cara*, concentrate solely on the man you are dining with.'

Not quite sure if she was supposed to laugh at the ridiculous image Nikos had constructed of the waiter muscling in on him, he diverted her with, 'What would you like to eat?'

Mia dutifully buried her attention on the menu. A different waiter arrived to take their order. Nikos delivered it in the clipped cool tone that did not encourage the waiter to linger.

'Talk to me,' he said abruptly once they were alone again.

Lifting up her face she asked, 'What about?'

'Anything—the wine.' He indicated to her glass.

Dutifully picking up her wine glass Mia sipped. 'Nice,' she said.

'Is that it?'

'Is this another lesson in social dining?' she dared.

'No.' He almost let a smile catch hold of his mouth. 'It is simply a request for you to extend your answer. You are Italian. I cannot believe you don't have a better opinion about wine than just *nice*.'

Be interesting, in other words. Well, OK, she could try to do that, Mia decided, relaxing back into her seat. 'Tia Giulia and I make our own wine from our own grapes,' she announced. 'It's just a hobby really, but our wine tastes easily as good as this very expensive wine…' she said with a wave of her glass. 'We pick and tread the grapes in the traditional manner with our skirts held up like so—' she gestured, unaware how entirely she had captured her audience '—and we laugh a lot—it is supposed to be good for the taste. If it is a good year, our neighbours will come to exchange other produce for bottles of our wine. *Tia* has some really wonderful old oak barrels in the cellar....'

Their first course arrived and Mia kept talking through it, taking a small forkful of sea bass laced with a delicious sauce she had never tasted before.

'Your life in Tuscany was very different from the one you're living now,' Nikos observed when she paused for a breath.

Mia nodded, eyes shadowing as she sat forward to pick up her glass. 'Do you miss Greece when you are away from it?'

'Not particularly,' he said. 'I fly in and out of Athens too often to miss it.'

'Family, then,' she probed.

'None.' The way he carefully veiled his eyes made Mia frown because she was almost certain she'd just hit a raw nerve. 'Tell me why you left it so long to contact Oscar.' As neatly as that he turned the conversation away from him and back on to her.

'Because I only discovered I had a father

this year—on my twenty-first birthday to be exact…'

She went on to explain about discovering Oscar, in between savouring forkfuls of food. She didn't notice that Nikos barely touched the food on his plate, or that he rarely removed his dark eyes from her face. She was not aware that he kept filling up her wine glass or that her tongue was loosening the more that she drank. By the time their dessert arrived she was feeling so mellow she even reached across the table to spoon up a sample of his untouched dessert and teased him with her laughing eyes as she placed the stolen morsel in her mouth.

'I have a sweet tooth.'

'Among other things,' he murmured oddly.

About to ask him what he meant by that—

'Do you want coffee?' he got in before her.

'And spoil the taste of the wine? *Grazie*, no,' she refused.

'Then if you've finished do you mind if we leave now?'

'Oh…' Mia tensed, her slender spine arching up on the sudden realisation that she'd talked his socks off all the way through the meal! It was no wonder he was wearing that blank expression on his face. 'I had lost track of how long we have been here…'

'And the restaurant has emptied,' Nikos pointed out dryly. 'We're the last ones here...'

Flickering a surprised glance around the empty tables she noticed the restaurant staff standing around, trying hard not to look impatient for them to leave. 'Why didn't you say something sooner?' she whispered from the depths of a sinking embarrassment.

'You were enjoying your meal. There was no need to rush.' With the merest glance in the waiter's direction he brought him rushing to his side. 'My companion's jacket,' he instructed, handing over a credit card. 'You have time to finish your wine,' he indicated smoothly to Mia, as if she would dare to take another sip!

'No.' She stood. 'I think I've had enough.' A flush of hot colour was burning her cheeks.

She wanted to die where she stood—deflate like a balloon and disappear altogether. She almost snatched her jacket from the waiter when he arrived with it, so eager to remove herself from here now that she could barely stop herself from doing it at a run.

The waiter was handing Nikos his credit card. Mia fumbled in her urgency to drag her jacket on and missed slotting her arm in the sleeve.

'Allow me...'

She froze as Nikos took the garment from her and politely held it open, ready for her to slip it on. Her hair became trapped inside the black satin and she used the need to release it as an excuse to keep her head lowered so no one could see how hot her face had gone.

Outside the cool night air hit her like an icy slap in the face and she shivered. Nikos placed a hand against her lower back to walk her towards his waiting car. A beep sounded as the locks sprang free and his hand guided her into her seat.

The car growled into life. It moved away from the curb with the sleek prowling grace of a hunting panther. As her gaze was drawn downwards to watch as his long fingers moved the car through its gears, she saw something that caught her breath in her throat.

'What—?' Nikos asked, so sharp he obviously did not miss anything.

'Nothing.' Dragging her eyes away from the black-and-gold insignia she'd spied on the dash, she tried to pretend that she had not seen it. Then, without any warning at all, she choked, 'I feel sick.'

The stunned silence which followed her announcement held for a second or two, then the car ground to a jerking halt. Nikos was out of it and striding round to yank her door open before Mia could do it for herself. Out in the night air again, she began to shiver so badly he must have felt compelled to offer a supporting arm around her shaking shoulders while she stood fighting a battle with nausea that had nothing to do with the amount of wine she had drunk.

Nikos did not know that though. He was cursing himself. He wished the hell he knew what he had been playing at back there, feeding her wine by the glassful to draw her out of her shell. What had he hoped to gain from it? An insight into what made his PA tick, or had his motives been fixed somewhere else?

'It's usually better to throw up and get it over with than to fight it,' he advised, trying to recall the last time he'd deliberately set out to get a woman drunk.

There had never been another time. He had never sunk this low before. She got to him and he didn't like it. She made him think, do and want things he did not want to think, do or want.

'I'm all r-right.' Making an effort to pull herself together, Mia stepped away from his supporting arm to stand by herself.

Letting his arm drop to his side he sighed, 'I'm—sorry.'

He was sorry? 'What for?'

'I should not have let you drink all that wine.'

'I can take my wine, Nikos Theakis,' Mia threw back. 'I am Italian. I grew up drinking wine. It was your car that made me feel sick. I hate it. I will walk the rest of the way—'

'What do you mean, my car made you sick?' Grabbing her arm as she went to walk away from him he pulled her to a halt.

Mia shivered. 'It is a Mario Mattea production car.'

'A limited edition,' Nikos confirmed. 'Only twenty of them were built. Most people would—'

'One for each year Mario Mattea has been married to my mother,' Mia whispered, then had to press her lips together as the nausea threatened to come back.

She couldn't believe she hadn't noticed the world-famous insignia before now! The two stylishly entwined gold letter *M*'s appeared on a million luxury products—on Mario Mattea's main claim to fame—his world-championship-class formula-one racing cars!

A glance at the low silver bonnet and a thick laugh broke from her throat. Wouldn't Mario just love it if he knew that one of his cars had almost ploughed her into the ground a few months ago!

Pushing off Nikos's hand, she started walking, needing to get as far away from that car as fast as she could. The nausea was churning up her stomach and her arms had wrapped themselves tight around her ribs. She'd lived twenty-one years in Italy and not once seen a Mattea car. Then she arrives in England, and on the very first day she'd almost had one toss her over its bonnet without realising the insult she would have been paying to herself!

'Explain.' Nikos caught up with her.

'Oscar slept with my mother, Gabriella, the night before he married Lillian,' she supplied in a cold, clipped voice. 'She returned to Italy—to her fiancé Mario Mattea and eventually married him.'

Nikos breathed what Mia assumed was the Greek way of expressing shock. 'So your mother is Gabriella Mattea…'

'Don't bother to fixate on it,' Mia sparked out. 'I do not recognise her as my mother. We do not communicate.'

'Slow down before you twist off those ridiculous high shoes,' he instructed impatiently, curling a set of long fingers around her arm.

'You have forgotten your car,' she muttered in the hopes that he would take the hint and leave her to walk home alone.

'And you've forgotten the rules of dating again,' Nikos responded coolly. 'I see mine to their door.'

'We did not have a date,' Mia denied. 'You hijacked me in the street.'

'Same rules apply.' Still holding on to her, his attention had diverted to the two streams of traffic moving up and down the street. He spotted a gap. His fingers tightened. 'Come on,' he said, 'let's cross while we can.'

Finding herself being hustled across the road, Mia was instinctively drawn to glancing both ways to check out the pace of the traffic for herself. Her eyes rested on his silver car standing abandoned against the curb a hundred metres away and she shivered, dragging her eyes away from it again. She hated the long, sleek, glossy power statement it made—the whole high-profile sparkle of the Mattea name. In Italy it meant glittering celebrity and untold wealth—much like the Balfour name did here, she likened, suddenly hating all of it.

'I'm surprised the press here hasn't picked up who your mother is,' Nikos murmured once they were safely on the opposite pavement.

'Oscar has been careful not to make the connection,' she revealed. 'Gabriella was still a Bianchi when he—knew her.' Bianchi being the only name Gabriella had ever allowed Mia to own. Did she care? No, she told herself. It was bad enough that everyone knew she was the result of a sordid one-night stand of one decadent parent, Oscar Balfour, without being linked to her other notoriously decadent parent, Gabriella Mattea, as well. 'Bianchi is a common name in Italy.'

They turned into the street on which their apartment block was situated. Once again Nikos slowed their pace. 'Why aren't you a Mattea?'

He just couldn't leave it alone! 'Why the sudden interest in my sleazy past?'

'It's not your sleaze, Mia, it's theirs,' Nikos pointed out.

Only slightly mollified by that response, Mia pulled in a tense breath. 'When Gabriella found out she was pregnant with me she tried to pass me off as Mario's child but she badly miscalculated,' she explained. 'Mario cannot have children apparently, and he certainly did not want some other man's child cluttering up his life, so he set her an ultimatum. She kept me and lost him, or she gave me up and kept him. You know the rest,' she concluded, tightening her grip on her ribcage as if trying to hug her bitter feelings in.

'The isolated farm in Tuscany,' Nikos confirmed, 'an aunt barely scratching out a living for you both, while your filthy-rich parents live their lavish lives... It has all the ingredients for a seventeenth-century costume drama about the underbelly of two glittering royal houses,' he described.

Mia pulled to a stop and swung on him. 'You would make a really good member of the paparazzi to listen to you,' she fired at him hotly, '*and* you would probably enjoy it!'

To her rising fury his mouth twitched out the beginnings of a smile.

'You think my life is amusing?'

'I think it's priceless.' The smile became a full white-toothed grin. 'So should you.'

Tossing her hair back, Mia glared up at him. His lean dark face was so disgustingly gorgeous she— 'I don't want to talk any more about it.' She swung away again, hating the hot sexual tension she could feel working away at her insides.

She set off walking. Nikos kept pace at her side. 'If you want my opinion, Mia…'

'I do not,' she clipped out.

'You should talk about it more often,' he continued anyway. 'You take yourself too seriously—and stop this!' He sighed, turning her back round to face him, then grimly prizing her arms away from her ribs and down to her sides, where her hands clenched into white-knuckle fists.

Nikos viewed them with exasperation. 'Body language is worth a thousand words,' he sighed out. 'Has it not occurred to you that if you don't care where you came from, then no one else will care?'

'Be brazen about it, you mean?'

'It's got to be better than clutching it to you like a grudge. Wake up and smell reality, Mia. Stop pitying yourself. You have a colourful past. So what? Without it you would not be here at all!'

Pitying herself? She wanted to say—how do you know what it feels like to be me? But that would be self-pitying so she pressed her lips together and said nothing and simmered a furious glare at him instead. His eyes were almost black in the darkness, flamed by the gold from the pooling street light. The same with the warm olive skin covering the taut beauty of his cheekbones, his nose, the darker shaded contours of his smooth, wide sensual mouth.

Something new charged up the atmosphere. It began with a small flicker of his long eye-lashes as he dropped his gaze to her mouth. He wanted to kiss her. Mia knew it with an instinct older than time itself. Her heart stopped beating, then started up again at a faster pace because— *Dio*, she wanted him too—so much.

He knew he was going to do it. He knew he

just couldn't hold back. She was beautiful, a warm, soft, achingly desirable creature with passion in her eyes and on her softly pulsing mouth.

Sliding his fingers into her hair, he stroked a fingertip along the smoothness of her extended throat. The blue of her eyes deepened to purple and her lips parted. He felt the growing rush of her blood flow into his own. She swayed even closer, a willing recipient of what was about to happen. Feeling like a man controlled by a magnet, Nikos kept totally still as she brought her mouth closer and closer to his.

A car drove past them sounding its horn noisily and they sprang apart like two tightly coiled springs breaking free from their restraints.

Dizzied by the pressure that had built up inside her, Mia stumbled backward a few steps at the same time that Nikos broke the grip he still held on one of her arms. Staring at him, feeling a sinking sense of confusion assail her, it all suddenly changed to a sense-crawling horror when she realised that she had been the one about to kiss him.

She spun away in a shaken, horrified need to escape what she'd almost done. The apartment's car park was only a few metres away. Walking across it, she was so anxious to punch in her security PIN so she could get inside before he could reach the doors that she keyed the numbers in the wrong order and had to cancel to begin the sequence again. His arm reaching across her shoulder to do the job for her drew sparks from her muscles as they pulled taut.

The door swung open. They stepped inside the lobby. Neither said another word to each other as the lift took them up to the top floor. Refusing to look into the mirrors, Mia glued her eyes to the lift's marble floor. She could *feel* his presence though, like a fierce wave of energy battering into her and her insides were fizzing so badly she could not even breathe.

The moment the doors opened she darted out of the lift to escape. 'Wait a minute, Mia.' His quiet voice pulled her to a stop halfway across the lobby. 'You've forgotten something.'

Narrow shoulders snapping with tension, she did not want to turn around but stiff pride made her do it. He was standing near the lift, his broad-shouldered posture somehow deceptively passive because, even with her non-existent experience, Mia was able to detect the prowling sexual pulse beat emanating from him. Wild butterflies were beating their wings in her stomach. Without being aware she was doing it, she brought her fingers together across her front in an anxious defensive pleat.

'What?' she prompted warily, and not for the life of her could she look at his face…

Nikos wondered how she would react if he offered to finish what they had started down in the street. She looked so damn beautiful standing there, trying hard not to show she was upset. And her innocence pounded at him like a bloody great barrier. It made him want to crash through it and just—

Just what?

Desire was one hell of an aphrodisiac when someone else was feeling it for you, he thought heavily. One unguarded look, the tempting thought of those anxious fingers touching his body, the sensual promise her lush parted mouth had offered him down in the car park… All it would take was a loosening of his self-control and the conflagration would happen and they might both gain some relief.

Shame Oscar stopped him from carrying through.

'Your manners,' he responded finally. 'It is usual to thank the guy that bought you dinner.'

It was like he'd reached out and cut her throat. So cool, so sardonic, he was even *still* in lecture mode. Mia drew her eyes shut as the whole wretched agony of the way he was treating her exploded like a firework of needle-hot sparks which turned to ice as they embedded themselves in her flesh.

'Thank you,' she delivered with stiff obedience, 'for such—a pleasant evening, *signor*.'

'My pleasure, *signorina*,' he returned, and even the supercontrolled Nikos Theakis could not stop the rueful twitch that took hold of his mouth.

He caught a glimpse of some of Oscar's arrogance in the way she nodded her head at him before she spun away on the heels of her ridiculously high shoes. Her chin was high, her shoulders back, her hair a glossy black stream of loose waves down her taut back. Not a single tremor showed in her body as she walked up to her door, keyed in her security code, then pushed open the door and stepped inside.

The door shut with an impressively controlled soft thud behind her. As if it was a sign that he could drop his guard—or whatever it was that was holding him—Nikos let his shoulders fall back against the wall behind him and closed his eyes.

Mia Bianchi was fast becoming the kind of recreational drug he never indulged in. The kind you only took on if you were looking for total loss of control of your life.

He needed a woman, Nikos decided grimly.

He should not have blown off the one he could have been seeing tonight, in favour of chasing after the one he could not have.

Opening his eyes on that lowering confession, mouth turned down at the corners as he dragged himself free of the wall, he speared a final glance at her closed door, then turned to stride back into the lift and stabbed a long finger at the button which would take him back to the ground floor.

Mia watched from her bedroom window as Nikos crossed the car park with the long loose-limbed stride of a man eager to depart. Duty done, she thought miserably. Annoying responsibility returned safely home, now he was going out to catch up on his real life. And he had his mobile phone clamped to his ear to find out where that life happened to be situated right now.

A woman?

Of course a woman, she told herself, reaching out to snap the blind shut so she could not see him any more.

CHAPTER FIVE

THE sound of her mobile chiming out its jingle brought Mia swimming up from the dark depths of the heavy sleep she had eventually tumbled into after tossing about restlessly for half of the night.

Stretching out a hand and groping the bed-side table to make contact with the flat black contraption, she tucked her arm back beneath the duvet and pushed the phone to her ear before mumbling, *'Ciao.'*

'It's Nikos,' he announced with his usual impatience. 'I have to go down to Hampshire and you're coming with me.'

Sitting up with a jolt, her sleepy eyes opened wide as saucers. 'Hampshire?' Mia echoed. 'W-what is in Hampshire—?'

'Work,' came the sardonic answer. 'Of the socialising kind.'

Still trying to cast off the heavy mists of sleep, Mia pushed the tumble of ebony curls off her face. 'But it's Saturday,' she remembered. 'I am supposed to be meeting—'

'I don't recall promising you would get your weekends free when you came to work for me,' Nikos rode roughshod over what she had been about to say. 'So whatever it is you have planned get out of it. I have to go out for a few hours but when I get back I will expect you to be ready to leave. You will need a dress—something formal.'

'Formal,' Mia repeated, stunned by the way he had just discarded her plans. 'H-how formal?'

'Bella-at-her-red-carpet-best formal,' he delivered dryly, referring to her wildly beautiful and glamorous supermodel half-sister. 'Do you have something like that to wear?' he then thought to ask.

Dragging herself to the edge of the bed and standing, Mia sent her mind's eye sweeping down the packed dress rail in the other bedroom. '*Sí*, I think so,' she mumbled. 'But— Nikos, I am not very good at these formal occasions,' she threw in anxiously. 'I don't think—'

'This is at Oscar's command, not mine,' he informed her with the cool thrust of a murderer plunging a knife into her chest. 'He wants you there to represent the family because no one else is available to attend. Do you want to call and tell him you're not up to taking on the responsibility—?'

Dio. 'No,' Mia surrendered heavily. 'I will come.'

'Good,' he approved. 'Pack an overnight bag because we will be staying. See you at one o'clock.'

He cut the connection before she could find the necessary brain cells to ask any questions. Sinking heavily back onto the bed, her fuzzy brain listed: Hampshire, a formal evening dress, an overnight bag. Be ready to go by one o'clock...

Then she was suddenly lurching into panic mode and using her mobile phone to ring her half-sister Sophie.

'What is happening this evening in Hampshire?' she wrung out urgently.

'Hampshire?' Sophie Balfour repeated. 'Oh, my...'

'What does this *oh my* mean?' Mia demanded, already feeling the chill of alarm skate down her spine.

'Is Nikos taking you there?'

'*Sí.*'

'Then take a brave pill before you go, sweetie,' her half-sister advised her. 'If you thought attending the Balfour Charity Ball was major-nervous-breakdown stuff, then you're in for a shock because Hampshire is huge.'

'Huge...' Mia whispered, grappling with the complicated idiosyncrasies of the English language when spoken with sarcasm like this. 'You will have to explain this *huge* to me too,' she begged.

'Ever heard of the D'Lassio brothers?'

'No.' Mia frowned. 'Should I have heard of them?'

'What kind of Italian are you that you've never heard of the two sexiest Italian tycoons out there?' Sophie sounded shocked. 'Santino D'Lassio is married to the absolutely gorgeous Nina Francis and works out of London. Alessandro D'Lassio is so single it's mind-boggling and works out of Milan. Each year they stage a cross-continent charity event to top all charity events. One takes place on their fabulous country estate in Hampshire, the other at their magnificent ancestry pile situated on the banks of Lake Como. The two events will be linked by satellite. Television stations and the paparazzi will be out in force. Pop stars, royalty, the megarich and the superfamous will be attending—you're going to love it like a bullet in the head,' Sophie predicted. 'And I bet Lois Mansell is pretty miffed that Nikos is taking you instead of her,' Sophie said.

As if someone had thrust an icy rod down her backbone, Mia tensed up. 'Who—who is Lois Mansell?'

'Check out this morning's paper,' her half-sister advised. 'She's the fabulous blonde captured wrapped around Nikos as they left a nightclub together last night.'

At one o'clock to the absolute second, Mia presented herself in the top-floor oval lobby with her weekend bag as per instructions, and the dress she had decided to wear this evening draped over her arm in a cream silk dress bag. She was wearing faded designer denims, a thigh-hugging black *Vive La Rock* T-shirt and fiercely high black designer shoes. She'd confined her hair loosely to her nape with a big shiny black clip and her make-up was light.

For casual, cool and in strict control of her emotions were the absolute keys to her standing here at all. Indeed she'd been a breath away from using the flu bug excuse right up until the moment she'd stepped out of her apartment door.

His apartment door opened and her heart gave a single heavy little thump as Nikos stepped out. He was dressed more casually than she'd ever seen him, in pale chinos and a dove-grey V-neck sweater worn over a pale blue-and-grey-checked shirt. Big, lean, dark and classy, Mia listed, and had to bite back a bitter grimace when her head gave her another image of him, dressed in a black dinner suit leaving a famous nightclub with a leggy blonde clinging like a blood-sucking limpet to his side.

Their eyes met for a second. Her throat felt so thick Mia found she needed to swallow but wouldn't allow herself the relief. Their murmured greetings crossed over each other. She was the one to break the eye contact, lowering her eyelashes and feeling like the ice woman inside.

'Here, let me take your bag…'

As he stooped to lift her canvas holdall from where it sat at her feet, Mia found herself staring at the top of his head where the black silky thickness of his hair was glossed by the hint of curls.

Curls Lois Mansell had no doubt enjoyed running her long limpet fingers through last night, Mia tormented herself with the image she'd evoked.

'Do you want me to take your dress bag…?'

'No—thank you,' she managed politely.

The lift arrived and, determined to maintain a professional detachment if it killed her to do it, Mia walked into it, then stood with her chin tilted down so she did not have to look at him as they travelled to the ground floor.

The tabloid newspaper which printed the photograph had headlined it with:

Is this the new blonde Greek billionaire Nikos Theakis has chosen to replace Lucy Clayton?

As for the rest of the article, which highlighted his penchant for leggy blondes and his low attention threshold, it had said it all as far as Mia was concerned. She'd finally acknowledged that it was time for her to learn to get over him, and if that meant not looking at him, then she was not going to look at him.

'Something wrong?' his deep voice drawled.

'Nothing,' she responded.

'If you're worrying about tonight, then—'

'I am not worrying about anything.' She walked out of the lift before he could say anything else.

It was only as he forged ahead of her to open the door that she noticed he carried no weekend bag for himself. Presuming he must have already put it in his car, Mia walked past him and out into the bright sunlight...only to go still when she saw a brand-new shiny red sports car—that only a total hermit would not recognise for what it was—waiting in the place of his silver Mattea.

Her icy cool started to falter. 'Y-you've changed your car.'

'I prefer not to put my passengers through mental torture,' he relayed drily.

As Mia walked up to the door he was holding open for her she caught a gleam in his eyes which told her he was waiting for her to make some kind of positive response because he had gone to this much trouble exclusively for her.

When she said nothing, he grimaced. 'You can thank me later,' he murmured, 'once you've recovered from your sulk because I spoiled your plans for today.'

It took Mia a minute to grasp that he was referring to her plans to meet with Sophie. They'd planned to go shopping and take in a movie but Nikos had not given her a chance to tell him that during his phone call this morning. Opening her mouth to tell him, she snapped it shut again. Let him think what the heck he liked. What she did with her free time was none of his business—as his was not any of hers.

'Seat belt,' he issued as he climbed in next to her, and the pleasant tone had disappeared from his voice, Mia noticed.

A few minutes later they were driving across the river towards Battersea. Mia tried not to watch the way he controlled his new car as if he had been driving it for years. It must be in his blood to know instinctively what to do in any given situation. She'd seen him at work too often not to be impressed with the way he could control most things with an ease that was so breathtakingly natural even those he was controlling did not notice he was doing it.

It was no wonder he was arrogant sometimes, a bit of a bully when he felt he needed to be. Incisive, *decisive*, he was used to being right so why not expect other people to just fall in line to his bidding?

After attempting to kick-start several conversation subjects to which she replied in crushing monotones, he issued a driven sigh. 'Quit the chilly sulk, Mia,' he told her, 'or I will turn this car around and take you back home again.'

Mia straightened in her seat. 'I am not sulking.'

'No?' Stopping at a set of traffic lights he turned to look at her—deep brown eyes, feathered with flashes of glinting gold, spun nerve ends alive across her taut profile. 'You remind me of a feral cat I once tried to befriend as a kid. One minute she was soft and coquettish and brushing her sleek body up against me, the next minute she had her claws in my neck and was spitting at me.'

'I have never brushed up against you!' she denied, then felt her cheeks flame when she recalled the way she'd moved towards him last night. 'Nor have I drawn my claws,' she added as a quick cover-up. 'And if I remind you of your friend the feral cat, then you remind me of our donkey,' she threw back, sparked into defending herself.

'Your—what?' he raked out.

'Tulio, our donkey,' she supplied. 'One minute he is beautifully relaxed and amenable, the next he acts as if he does not occupy the same planet as everyone else.'

'You're accusing *me* of being moody?' Nikos delivered across the gap separating them.

Mia fixed her gaze on the traffic lights. 'I cannot predict how you are going to speak to me from one minute to another. Tulio is the same. Only he does not speak—he just gives me the evil eye to say I don't feel like being nice to you any longer, and so he isn't.' She added a self-explanatory shrug. 'The lights have changed colour,' she pointed out.

'A donkey,' he breathed, steering the car into a right turn, then accelerating up the street. *'Grazie, cara,'* he said with grim sarcasm, and swung the car off the street into a small car park by the banks of the river, killed the car engine and climbed out.

Mia hugged a pleased smile to herself as she watched him stride around the car bonnet with his golden good looks pronounced by the savage look on his face.

So she'd just insulted him and ruined his day.

Good, she thought, because he had ruined hers too with his nocturnal activities splashed all over the papers!

Did she have the right to be angry about that?

She did not *care* if she had no right—she just did!

She hated him. She hoped Lois Mansell was the worst lover he had ever bothered to bed. And she was not jealous! she told herself furiously, she was just—

He pulled open her door for her with more angry strength than the beautifully designed piece of equipment required. As she carefully manoeuvred her high-heeled shoes over the sill of the car, his grim impatience with her transferred to the long fingers he clamped around her arm to help straighten her up. Arriving in front of him with more impulse than was necessary, she ended up almost flattened against him, which shocked her enough into glancing up.

Their eyes clashed—his slightly narrowed and glinting golden warning shots for her to take care what she did or said next, hers sparking with bright blue defiance which dared him to make one of his cold, cutting comments gauged to knock her back down to size.

But he went for a different kind of attack. He relaxed the corners of his hard, clipped mouth, slid a hand around her exposed nape, then lowered his head and captured her mouth with a hard, hot, plundering kiss!

Astonishment thrilled through Mia. It was so shockingly unexpected and so shockingly intimate she was unable to do anything but just let him explore the contours of her mouth with a sensual fluency that glued her to the spot.

Knocked completely for six she staggered dizzily when he lifted his head again. Breathless and shaking and unable to focus on anything, she just stared up at him through a thick misty glaze.

'Different mood, *cara*,' he purred down at her like his very own feral cat. 'I sincerely hope that Tulio is not so adventurous.'

His meaning shocked a gasp from Mia. As if he felt he deserved her reaction Nikos nodded his dark head, then let go of her and turned abruptly to glare at the young man who had approached them without her being aware of it.

'Get the bags out of the boot and give them to my pilot, then take the car back,' he instructed, tossing the keys at the other man.

Still much too stunned to take in the bit about his pilot, Mia slung a swift glance at whoever it was Nikos was talking to, saw it was the man from accounts she had lunched with yesterday and also saw that his eyes were standing out in shock.

Heat poured into her face like a scorching flame. It was bright sunny daylight, and Nikos Theakis had just kissed her full on her mouth in front of another member of his staff!

'You—you did that on purpose!' she hissed at him shakenly.

Nikos claimed one of her hands and walked her away from the car. 'He needed showing where he stands with you.'

'Stands with me?' Mia gasped out. 'I don't understand this *stands with me*,' she told him, having to hurry to keep up with his long stride.

'He was the date that stood you up last night.'

'He was not my date!'

'He was your date,' he insisted. 'And I have just made my point.'

'Will you please explain what it is you are talking about?' Tugging hard on her captured hand she pulled them both to a stubborn stand-still in front of a white building with glass entrance doors. Hot, mortified, her kissed lips burning and feeling shockingly pumped up, still she made herself glare up at him.

He looked down at her, as cold and haughty-looking as she had ever seen him. And *his* lips were not burning! 'I saw you talking with him in my foyer yesterday at lunch,' Nikos confessed. 'By the time he comes out of his shock far enough to read the message I've just given him, he will understand that you are out of bounds from now on if he wants to keep his job.'

Sent totally, utterly breathless by the ruthless steel trap his mind must be, Mia could not get another single word out. She twisted her head to look towards the red sports car where, sure enough, the man from accounts was still standing next to as if in shock.

Her insides shuddered. 'You—you set me up for that kiss in front of him,' she whispered, finally beginning to catch on as to why that particular employee of his had been roped in to deal with his car.

'No, Tulio did that. Until Tulio put in an appearance I'd decided that merely seeing you going off to spend a weekend with me was going to be enough to put him off thinking he could try coming on to you again. Tulio upped the ante.'

Tugging her into motion again he sent the glass doors swinging open and walked them into the building, then kept her anchored to his side as he spoke to a receptionist standing behind the desk. Fizzing with fury Mia wanted so badly to deny what he'd assumed, but she knew that she could not do that without exposing the real reason why she had gone out last night, and nothing was *ever* going to make her admit the truth to him now!

So she stood simmering beside him with her eyes on a level with his wide muscular shoulder, and only began to take notice of her surroundings when she happened to focus through a window and saw the helicopter glinting in the bright sunlight on what looked like a concrete jetty jutting out into the Thames.

Her fingernails bit tense crescents into Nikos's palm. She had never travelled in a helicopter before, and she was not sure she wanted to travel in one now.

Nikos tried not to wince as her fingernails bit into his flesh as he signed the necessary documents and felt alive for the first time in two long miserable weeks. A fire was burning deep down in his abdomen. He didn't know how she had managed to do this to him, this black-haired, long-legged, curvy fiery witch, but she did do it to him. If he had been standing in the middle of a wilderness he would be howling now like a mating wolf.

He'd warned Oscar. He'd warned Mia. He'd even warned himself. But it had taken a donkey named Tulio to set his natural hunting instinct free from the restraints he had placed around them. Turning back to the glass doors he trailed his captive outside again. His new sports car was nowhere to be seen now. Grimacing at the delight he could imagine its young driver was

enjoying—the young fool's damn consolation
prize—Nikos turned them towards the jetty on
which his helicopter was awaiting them.

Mia was forced to endure his help as he
helped her up the steps into the plush cream
leather interior, with the bristling impatience of
a man who believed he had the right to hustle
her around.

The impression stung like acid through the
layers of her skin as she chose a seat on the
other side of the cabin and sat down. She
refused to look at him as he folded his long
frame into the seat farthest away from her. If
two people wished to announce they were at
war, then their seating choices flagged the battle
line.

The door slid shut. Rotor blades began to
move. The angry butterflies playing havoc with
her insides altered to anxious tingles as she felt
the contraption lift off the ground. As her heart
dipped alarmingly she watched with wide eyes
and, in what felt like only seconds, she found
herself staring down at the river which looked
like a silver ribbon glinting in the sun.

He did not speak. She did not speak. But she
could feel the fierce heat of his mood reaching
out towards her across the empty gap.

And her lips were still burning so hotly from
the kiss she found she just had to try to cool

them with the moist tip of her tongue. Her mouth suddenly came alive with the taste of him. Shocked that a kiss could leave such an intimate residue behind, she slammed her tongue against the back of her teeth and refused to let it move again.

'Drink—?'

Mia forced herself to look at him, only to feel a strange heavy weight descend across her chest. He looked different again—as in *dangerously* different. His lounging posture in the corner of the plush leather seat, with his long legs stretched out in front of him, yelled cool, calm arrogance at her, yet his half-narrowed eyes and the glint emitting from them warned of something new lurking around inside him, as if he'd flung on yet another change of mood.

Passion-desire, she named it, without knowing how she recognised either thing. Her eyes dropped to his mouth, his wide sensual mouth. Could he taste her as she could still taste him—?

Mia shook her head and turned to look at the horizon where the built-up city had begun to thin out and the earth below them was slowly turned into a thousand shades of green as they flew over countryside.

Across the cabin, Nikos was talking on his

mobile phone. In front of her, hidden behind a bulkhead, some invisible person was flying them to—she knew not where because she had forgotten to ask where they were staying.

A short while later they began to sink downwards. Mia saw a series of slated rooftops forming the shape of a large country house standing in the centre of sweeping clipped green lawns sloping down to a tiny lake.

As they settled on the grass a short walk away from the creamy painted walls of the house, she assumed that it must be a hotel. And only realised her mistake when Nikos led the way in through the front door and she heard him greet a smartly dressed man with thick greying hair, before strolling over to a side table to begin sifting through the small pile of letters she could see waiting there.

'This is a house,' she murmured, pausing to look around the light and airy hallway.

Nikos threw her a glance. 'What did you think it was?'

'A hotel.'

His smile was more of a grimace. 'This is my home—or the one I use at weekends if I'm in England.'

'Sophie did not mention it.'

'Why would she?'

Eyelashes flickering away from the sturdy

staircase built of rich golden oak which took up central position, Mia looked at him, then away again.

'No reason,' she said, except that Sophie always seemed to know everything, so the fact that she did not know Nikos had a country house in Hampshire seemed—odd. 'How many homes do you have?' she asked curiously.

'Too many, probably,' he mocked. 'I don't like hotels,' he explained. 'I prefer my own space.'

There was something in the way that he'd said that, which made Mia frown as she studied his face. It told her nothing, and he appeared completely relaxed, yet—

Someone came in through the open front door then, making her turn about. It was the man Nikos had greeted as they'd arrived here and he was carrying her holdall and dress bag.

'This is Lukas.' Nikos made the introductions. 'Lukas keeps the house running smoothly. If you need anything while you're here, Lukas can usually provide it. Miss Balfour, Lukas,' he said.

'Good afternoon, Miss Balfour,' Lukas greeted her politely. 'I will take your things up to your room, then organise some refreshment.'

He strode off towards the stairs, leaving Mia chewing her bottom lip as she watched him go.

It was all very easy, very polite. Very much as she'd become used to at Balfour Manor, yet it was contrarily nothing like that estate. Balfour Manor was vast in comparison to this house, with masses of heavy panelling, and long galleried walkways steeped in priceless works of art and stunning antiques. This place had soft cream walls and a gentle, more classical feel to it.

She liked it.

'Take a look around while I finish reading through these,' Nikos invited, his attention back on his stack of mail.

Wandering off, Mia discovered that all the doors stood open already as if in invitation for her to step into each room. The first one she chose turned out to be a beautiful living room with squashy gold velvet sofas and chairs. A grand piano stood in front of a pair of French windows situated at one end of the room.

'Do you play?' she asked Nikos as she walked out of the room again.

'I used to. I don't have much time these days.'

Wondering why he sounded so indifferent to possessing such a wonderful gift, she crossed the hall to the other side and discovered a creamy book-lined study with a large desk filling the window and olive-green furnishings.

Stepping out again she saw that Nikos had

finished with his letters and was now studying her. A frisson ran down through her body. Conscious suddenly that they appeared to be alone here apart from Lukas, Mia wasn't sure if she was comfortable with the arrangement, though she tried not to show it.

'How—how far are we away from the D'Lassios' place?' she asked him.

'Five minutes by helicopter, twenty minutes by car. Do you want to see the rest of the house or are you ready for something to eat and drink?'

She didn't know what she wanted to do. Her fingers were restlessly pleating together and unpleating again, and for some reason she felt very unsure of her ground where his mood was concerned right now. He was relaxed, yes. He was being very pleasant. But there was something different about him that made her want to—

What—?

Back off? Run?

He was not offering to show her to her room, which was usually the first thing people did with a guest who was staying overnight. Not that she *wanted* him to show her to her room, Mia told herself quickly. But—

But *what*?

Exasperated with herself, she decided her

best choice while she was feeling so unsettled was, 'I think I would like to look around some more.'

With a nod of his dark head he led the way towards the back of the house. Half an hour later she'd been shown an all-purpose gym and an indoor swimming pool, a very elegant dining room, two more less formal sitting rooms and a huge rear garden that was a blaze of colour from the early summer flowering bulbs. Not once did Nikos rest so much as a hand on her, yet she quivered inwardly all the time as if he was threatening to do it.

It was the fault of the kiss, she told herself. The knowledge that he had come at her out of nowhere with it and so could easily come at her out of nowhere with something else.

He was volatile—unpredictable. The kind of man who was a law to himself. He fascinated and unnerved her in equal measures, and her awareness of his close proximity played like a bow across the taut string of her nerves, which in turn kept every sense she possessed honed on him.

'It's a very big house for just Lukas to look after,' she remarked eventually. 'You have no other staff?' She hadn't seen a single other person.

'Plenty, but they know not to be around when I'm here,' Nikos said.

Because, as he'd already said, he liked his own space—which should not surprise her since she was able to live in the service flat at his London apartment because he usually kept it empty.

His mobile phone rang then and, after taking the call, he murmured, 'Excuse me, I have to deal with this,' and strode off towards his study, talking in Greek.

It was like being let off for good behaviour. Mia felt herself almost deflate with relief. Working closely with him was taxing. *Fighting* with him was taxing! But being treated to a whole hour of his graciously polite side had worn her out!

How did he manage to switch his moods on and off like a light switch? How did he go from impatient boss to hot, angry kisser with serious possessive tendencies that made her insides flip over to amiable companion?

Passionate, pre-calculating, domineering and dangerous, she listed, quivering despite not wanting to react at all.

What mood was he going to treat her to next? The urban sophisticate wearing his social mask while a Balfour hung on his arm?

He was tying her emotions in knots with his quick-change mood swings. She needed something to do to take her mind off him.

Fortunately Lukas appeared as if by magic to offer her the promised refreshment. 'It's such a beautiful day, perhaps you would enjoy sitting out on the terrace? I'm sure Mr Nikos will not be long.'

Mr Nikos could take as long as he liked, Mia thought as she followed Lukas across one of the rear sitting rooms and outside. The moment she relaxed into a cushioned chair and the warmth of the sun touched her face, she felt homesick for Tuscany and Tia Giulia's peeling pink farmhouse and the rickety wooden furniture they used like an extension of the old-fashioned kitchen throughout the long summer months.

Lukas unfurled a huge canvas umbrella, suddenly dousing her in shade. She knew he'd meant well but she'd been happier to close her eyes and bake for a little while, something she had not had the opportunity to do since she'd arrived in England.

Just something else she missed about Tuscany.

'Something cool to drink or would you prefer coffee or tea?' enquired Lukas.

A sudden imp inside her made her want to demand a large shot of vodka, just to see how Lukas would react. She had never, ever tasted vodka but the house, Lukas and all of this polite care and attention did not fit with the cool, tough, impersonal if-I-can-do-it-myself-I-will nature of Nikos Theakis.

'Something cool,' she said meekly, smiling wryly to herself.

'Coffee for me, Lukas,' a third voice instructed.

Nikos strode out of the house and into the sunshine, then paused for second, lifting up his face as if he'd missed the sun too. His sweater had gone and he'd rolled back the sleeves of his checked shirt, revealing strong muscled forearms smattered lightly with fine black hair that made his skin look deeply tanned.

For a timeless moment Mia was held transfixed by his sheer bronzed beauty. A telling little flame flickered into life low down.

Then he tilted his chin down again and she dragged her eyes from him, feeling shaken inside and momentarily defenceless against these surges of attraction she kept on experiencing.

'They're going to slap a no-fly zone over the D'Lassio estate for the evening to stop the uninvited press from flying overhead,' he was telling Lukas, 'so can you make sure my pilot knows we need to leave to arrive before seven o'clock?'

With a nod Lukas left them alone on the terrace. Mia fixed her eyes on the garden where an elegant Greek goddess stood gently pouring water from an urn into a circular pond. So tranquil, she thought, when there was nothing tranquil about the man who must have had the pool and the goddess positioned there.

'So, what do you think?' He came to take the seat beside her, lazed back and stretched out his long legs.

'About the house? You must already know that it's very beautiful.'

'I purchased it last year from a business acquaintance, who needed some heavy cash fast,' he imparted casually. 'The idea was to sell it on but the current housing market made me decide to hang on to it for a while.'

'That explains it, then,' Mia murmured.

He turned his head to look at her. 'Explains what?'

'Did Lukas come with the house?' she responded with a question of her own.

'Yes,' he confirmed, and she nodded her head.

'The decor and the furnishings?'

His eyes started to narrow, and Mia felt that needling spark of electricity filter into the air. She had to moisten her lips with the tip of her tongue before she could go on. 'Your—stamp is not visible here.'

'Stamp,' he prompted.

'This is a—how do you say it…quintessential—? *Sí*, this is a quintessential model of an Englishman's country home.'

'What do you know about quintessential Englishmen?' Nikos laughed. 'You're a Tuscan farm girl with a donkey called Tulio for a best friend.'

'I have half-English blood,' Mia defended that comment.

'For all you know I might have half-English blood too,' Nikos tossed back.

Widening her blue eyes, she asked, 'Do you—?'

'No,' he conceded. 'But you couldn't know that. You're making assumptions about me without being in possession of all the facts. That's dangerous around me, *cara*.'

And Mia knew he was right. Then again, everything felt as if it had a dangerous element to it since she'd woken up this morning.

And when she could not manage to break eye contact with him, Mia knew it was getting worse.

CHAPTER SIX

MIA turned to look at herself in the full-length mirror and felt the now almost-permanent quiver going on low in her stomach quicken like mad.

The dress had once belonged to Bella. She'd spent half the morning shortening the long flow of its near-sheer iced-blue silk skirt. But it was the rest of the dress that made her senses quicken. The strapless style of the bodice draped lovingly around the thrusting shape of her breasts, then went on to hug each slender curve of her body with band after band of exquisitely intricate pleating all the way down to her thighs before the sheer silk flowed to her feet, elevated by the daintiest pair of crystal-studded high-heeled mules.

'Oh, my,' she breathed, stealing the expression Sophie had used on the phone that morning because it suddenly made a whole lot of sense.

Sparkling crystal droplets danced amongst the tight pleating, accentuating the shape of her body when she moved or even as she breathed. She'd coiled her hair into a loose pleat at her nape and her skin glowed smooth gold against the pale blue of the gown. A fabulous teardrop diamond necklace, given to her by Oscar, rested on its fine gold chain just above the sloping fullness of her breasts, and matching earrings sparkled at her ears. She had hoped to look elegant and sleek and sophisticated but what she'd seemed to have achieved was—alluringly sensual. She even felt sensual, in places she did not dare think about in case she made herself blush.

But she was chewing on her rose-coloured lip gloss and frowning uncertainly because she was just discovering that it was one thing to imagine herself dressing like this to impress a certain man, but it was quite a different sensation to realise she was seriously shocking herself.

Nikos was standing in the hall talking into his mobile phone when Mia appeared at the top of the staircase. As he glanced up and caught sight of her, the deep base tones of his voice stopped midsentence and he froze, his dark eyes flaring momentarily before he hooded them over with his long eyelashes, his gaze running in a slow sweep that allowed him to take in every sleek curvaceous inch.

Theos, I'm in trouble, was the only thought

he was able to register as a familiar heat flared low in his groin and somehow managed to mess with his breathing at the same time.

Then he became aware that he still held his phone to his ear and he turned his back on her while he finished the call and, at the same time, grabbed a tight mental grip on his rampaging libido.

This weekend is about *work*, he reminded himself.

Yeah, tell that to the kiss you can still taste.

Just watching the way he'd shut down his expression and how his strong jaw had clenched before he turned away was enough to tighten the knot of anxiety toying with Mia's stomach. He'd done it again, and beaten her up with his silent criticism. She didn't know whether to get angry or to weep.

She'd reached the last step before he turned around again, wearing his cool urban face. 'My apologies,' he said. 'Something urgent Petros needed to discuss with me before we left.'

He was walking towards her as he spoke, the absolute epitome of gorgeous handsome man about town in a formal dinner suit again.

'You look fabulous,' he delivered lightly. 'Love the dress.'

Mia managed a small tense smile in response.

'Do you have no coat, a shawl or something?'

Offering a shake of her head, she answered, 'The evening is quite warm.'

In truth, she had forgotten to bring anything like a shawl with her, but she was not going to admit that to this man who was floating a final glance over her before he gave a curt nod of his sleek dark head.

'Let's get going, then.'

Brisk, businesslike, firing on all pistons, Mia described as she walked beside him towards the front door. He did not need to say it out loud to remind her that this was all about work. Networking the social scene while pretending to enjoy themselves. Putting the Theakis name out there where it would be remembered, and remembering people he thought might be useful to him at some future date.

She wanted to ask him if she got paid overtime rates, but decided against setting the evening with a sarcasm that was bound to annoy him.

As they circled down over the D'Lassio estate, Mia was genuinely stunned by its palatial splendour, even with Balfour Manor to use for comparison. Balfour was built on more traditional lines with the patina of age to soften its sturdy grey stone walls, whereas this house was designed to look more like a Roman villa with a central courtyard and formal gardens fanning out from three sides of the house. The front of the house was mainly rolling green parkland split by a long sweeping drive. A makeshift car park to one side of the drive was already glinting due to the dying sun on the lines of cars.

Mia counted six helicopters parked up on the other side of the driveway and, as they swooped lower, she caught sight of two swimming pools, one outdoors and one contained beneath a dome of glass. Two television crews, and what felt like a thousand photographers, waited to record their arrival. The moment she saw them her heart started beating way too fast.

'Switch the Balfour smile on, *glikia mou*,' Nikos instructed softly as he helped her down the helicopter steps.

Obediently Mia switched on her smile. Camera shutters began clicking wildly and flashbulbs lit up the fading light. Nikos maintained his grip on one of her hands as they walked the media gauntlet on a thoughtfully laid carpet of artificial grass. Behind them the helicopter set its rotor blades moving again. A flurry of questions were being called out and a microphone was pushed into her face.

'Good evening, Miss Balfour, would you tell us which designer made your gown?'

Surprised to find herself staring directly into the lens of a television camera, Mia answered without thinking until it was too late to wonder if the world-famous Italian designer wanted his name given to this particular gown since it was at least twelve months old.

'Buona sera, signorina.' The sound of her native tongue calling out to her sent Mia's head swinging the other way, directly into a second television camera. 'Signor Valencia knows how to make the most out of a sensational figure, heh?' The interviewer had already picked up the dress designer's name. 'Will you take a moment to tell Italy what it is like for a Tuscan farm girl to discover she is the daughter of such a wealthy Englishman?'

The question came without warning. The camera zoned close on her face. Her fingers tensed, stretched, then pleated tightly in between Nikos's long fingers, and a warm flush of self-consciousness spread across her face while he just stood there beside her, smiling coolly, waiting for her to give a response.

It was a test, yet another lesson for her that he was letting her learn how to handle. Tutor and pupil at work in the classroom of life.

'*Sì… Grazie… Buona sera, Italia…*' Somehow she managed to keep her smile in place and come up with a reasonably intelligent comment about the differences between her old life and her new life.

'Love your voice, Mia!' someone else tossed at her in English. 'Very sexy. I could listen to you all night! What do you think, Nikos?'

Nikos just smiled and started them moving, thinking *sexy* did not begin to describe those dark throaty earth tones she used whenever she conversed in her natural language.

Dipping his dark head he murmured, 'You handled that well. Now let's see if we can get you through the rest of the evening without you making a bolt for the kitchens.'

'*Non capisco,*' Mia responded coolly, refusing to acknowledge the taunt about her well-documented bolt into the bowels of the kitchens the night of the Balfour Charity Ball.

Nikos gave a soft laugh and swapped his grip on her hand for an arm strapped across her back so he could hustle her in front of him into the house.

The next half an hour passed by in a whirl of first-time introductions that more camera crews recorded moment by moment. By the time she was given a chance to draw in a proper breath again, Mia was feeling dazed.

'You could have warned me,' she complained to Nikos.

'Forewarned, there was a chance you might do a runner,' he said, catching up two glasses of champagne and handing one to her.

'This place is amazing,' she changed the subject, glancing up at a high vaulted ceiling around which a cantilevered glass walkway seemed to stay up there by will alone.

'Santino likes to impress us with his structural engineering skills,' Nikos murmured dryly.

'I thought the D'Lassios were media moguls.' Mia frowned.

'Been doing your homework?'

Lifting her chin, she said, 'To improve my education is the reason why I am here with you, is it not?'

The direct challenge. Nikos arched an eyebrow because he had not expected her to make it. Like a fool playing a very dangerous game he held on to her deep blue eyes and piled the pressure on the constant tug of sexual awareness that was always present between them now.

She looked away first.

'Come on,' he said, 'let's move on to where the real action is.'

The *work* angle of action, Mia saw the moment they stepped inside a vast reception room already crammed with high-end glittering people. The networking started almost straight away. Nikos kept her at his side as he walked the room, rarely needing to make an effort to gain attention because people were more eager to meet him. It was the quality of the man and his billionaire kudos, his entrepreneurial brilliance, his stunning good looks and his casually presented charm. He handled people with a low-key edginess that made them work all the harder to earn themselves an impressed glance or an approving smile.

Smooth, Mia described as she soaked him in like the rest of them.

Then he ruined it for her when he turned to her and said, 'OK, this is where I leave you on your own for a while.'

Like a kick in the gut she instantly turned as white as parchment. Nikos released a sigh, catching her by the shoulders and turning her to face him.

'All you have to do is circulate and listen. If you know what they're talking about, join in. If you don't know what they're talking about, then ask questions,' he relayed as if it was really that simple. 'People don't mind being asked questions. In fact, they like to show off their knowledge. What they don't like is someone pretending to know what they're talking about when they don't. OK?'

Pressing the tremor out of her lips Mia nodded.

'And you're a Balfour,' he reminded her. 'The people here know you are a Balfour and they're going to just love to welcome you into their group on the strength of your name alone. In fact it's going to be them hoping to impress you so you will remember them to Oscar.'

'Not to you?'

'To me too,' Nikos agreed. 'If they ask you anything too personal shoot them down the way you like to do to me,' he went on. 'You have spirit, Mia, use it to your advantage. Always be polite. Always be aware of how much you're drinking. I will come and find you in, say, half an hour when we are due to go into dinner.'

Glancing down at the fine silver watch circling her wrist which Tia Giulia had bought her for her last birthday, she said, 'OK,' with only a tiny scared tremor showing in her voice.

Nikos heard it though and released a sigh.

'It's OK—really,' she said and straightened her shoulders. 'This is work—yes? I have to treat it that way.'

Still he hesitated, giving her the impression he wanted to say something else, and for some reason Mia found herself holding her breath.

Then he instructed, 'Don't bolt,' and walked away.

For the next half-hour Mia braved the sharp jaws of socialising. Like Nikos had said, it was easier than she expected because people did recognise her instantly and it tended to be them drawing her into their conversation rather than her needing to butt in.

Nikos wished he'd found it easy to walk away from her but he hadn't. He felt as if he'd abandoned a puppy on the fast lane of a motorway. But he needed to speak to some people about Lassiter-Brunel. During Mia's research exercise she had—admittedly unwittingly—exposed some business issues that were bothering him. OK, he reasoned, so he had pulled out of the deal they were trying to broker, but he'd done that for personal reasons. It was only this morning when he had gone back to the office to look through Mia's file that he had picked up on other things that troubled him.

She was good at ferreting, he acknowledged with an inner smile. But other colleagues in the same business might not have a ferret that looked so beautiful Brunel would let his professional guard slip to the point anyone would question whether he was as reputable as he made out.

Hearing himself using Mia's choice of word

made Nikos grimace at the same moment that a set of slender long fingers coiled around his arm. 'So you've been landed with Oscar's little cuckoo,' a mocking voice purred.

Glancing down Nikos found a smile for the beautiful but dangerous socialite-cum-gossip-columnist Diana Fischer who'd sidled up against him.

'Who would have believed Oscar could be such a deliciously secretive dark horse,' she went on. 'Perhaps it's as well that the scandal broke after poor Lillian departed to the afterlife. Imagine her horror if she'd been here to discover that the man she had been married to for twenty years had still been busy sowing his wild oats right up to and beyond their marriage.'

She was fishing for knowledge, timing details, that Nikos was not going to reveal. Setting his teeth together behind the relaxed line of his mouth, he drawled, 'Still enjoying playing the heartless bitch, Diana?'

'*I'm* heartless?' Her lovely green eyes opened wide. 'Tell me, Nikos, how many hearts have you broken since you became sexually active?'

'I was referring to your lack of respect for the dead.'

'I adored Lillian,' Diana declared. 'Everybody did. I thought I was being sympathetic towards her.' She pouted up at him. 'After all, who *would* want to find out that her husband had been laying into another woman?'

'Remind me,' Nikos murmured, 'why is Lance in the process of divorcing you?'

'Oh.' The luscious pout became pronounced. 'That was so below the belt, Nikos.'

Nikos released a dry laugh. Diana was a bitch and a brazen one but at least she never pretended to be anything else. He liked that about her—so long as she kept her barbs out of Oscar and his daughters.

Or one particular daughter, he amended, unable to stop himself from glancing across the room to hunt her down. He caught sight of her dark head in amongst a group of younger people and wasn't sure he liked the odd stinging sensation that ran down his front.

'The cuckoo is different from the other seven, isn't she,' Diana prodded lightly, following his gaze. 'She's so shy and reserved—just look at the way she's blushing at whatever Joel Symons is saying to her…'

Nikos was looking.

'She doesn't have a clue how to deal with people like us.'

'Like us?' Nikos was curious enough to pick up on the comment.

'Well, we've already established that I'm a

heartless bitch and you're a ruthless heart-breaker. And there is a room full of both those types here tonight. Elegant, bored, social spinners,' she extended candidly. 'Men with their egos in their wallets and their pants, and women with theirs in the exact same two places—and I meant in the men's,' she made clear. 'The cuckoo stares at us all as if we are aliens and I don't really blame her. Think what it must have been like for her to be launched like a bomb into Balfour society after spending all of her life halfway up a mountain, growing plants.'

'And perhaps she recognises that she's sauce for tongues like yours,' Nikos offered up.

And realised suddenly that he was right. Mia was not overwhelmed by the greatness of the elevated company her new life had thrown her into the midst of; she was overwhelmed by her own notoriety as Oscar Balfour's shockingly exposed illegitimate child.

'Do me a favour, Diana,' he said quietly. 'Keep your barbs out of Mia.'

'And you will do what for me?' she shot back.

Leaning down Nikos brushed a light kiss to one of her smooth cheeks. 'Respect you,' he murmured and walked away.

Mia saw the kiss and wondered what the name of that particular blonde was. He had beautiful blondes coming out of his pockets, she decided acidly, thinking of Lois Mansell, who he had been with just last night.

She pitied the one he'd just kissed and walked away from, she decided as she turned and strode off in the opposite direction. For there was one lesson Nikos had already taught her which stopped her short of being jealous of the new blonde and the kiss—he left with the woman he arrived with and saw her safely back to her own front door.

Or her bedroom door in her case tonight.

Or inside the bedroom door if it was anyone else.

A hand caught her wrist as she was about to continue through the open doors onto the pool terrace. For a brief second she thought it was Nikos and a wry smile curved her mouth as she turned her head with the intention of telling him the half an hour was not yet up.

But the smile died along with her sinking heart when she found herself staring into the cold silver eyes of Anton Brunel.

'I want words with you,' he informed her thinly.

'I don't think so.' Trying to pull free from his grip, her wrist hurt when he tightened his hold on it. 'Let go of me!' She frowned at him in contemptuous surprise.

'Not until I get some answers from you.'

Pulling her away from the doorway, he swung her into a corner of the room behind a giant palm plant. 'Right,' he said, pushing his handsome face up close to hers. 'You owe me a bloody explanation as to what the hell you think you're playing at, telling lies about me to Theakis!'

'I did not lie about you,' Mia denied, wincing when his hard fingers crunched the tender bones in her wrist.

'You spent that whole lunch turning me on with your sexy-eyed promises, then you told *him* it was *me* coming on to *you*!'

'You live in a strange place in your head, *signor*, if you truly believe what you just said,' Mia retorted scornfully, still trying to get away from him and glancing over the top of his blocking shoulder to see if anyone had noticed the way he'd cornered her like this.

It came as a shock to realise that he'd chosen his spot carefully because the palm plant virtually sealed them off from view.

Then she gasped when he pushed in on her, his body pressing her back against the wall. 'Listen to me,' he rasped. 'I want you to tell that jealous bastard the truth! You came on to me! You offered yourself up over the damn lunch table, and if I took the bait, he only has you to blame. I don't see why I should take the flack and lose the best investment deal I had going for my company because you like to play sex games across a table!'

His face was so close to hers that she was breathing in the alcohol from his angry breath.

'I would not play sex games across anything with you,' Mia whipped back, shuddering with distaste. 'And if you *don't* release me from this corner I will start shouting for help!'

'No, you won't,' he jeered. 'You're a Balfour, and too damn scared of making a scene here. Theakis won't like it. Darling daddy won't like it.'

'But I am not making the scene—you are! Now—let—me—go!'

With an angry tug she managed to yank her wrist free. As he went to grab hold of her again, she pushed at his body with her two clenched fists and enough angry strength to make him stagger back a small step, giving her just enough space to slither around him and get away.

Shaking inside with anger and reaction, she hurried out onto the pool terrace. Scared that he might be following her but determined not to look back and check, she made for the first group of people she saw standing by the swimming pool, and with a deep breath to calm her unsteady breathing, she ventured close enough for them to notice her, and smiled gratefully when they widened the circle to invite her to join in.

Did she do the things Anton Brunel had accused her of doing? Her eyes glazed with the agonised knowledge that she might have done without knowing she was even doing it. But did not knowing make her any less guilty? Hadn't Nikos accused her of doing the same thing to the waiter at the restaurant last night?

What was she, some kind of unwitting man-teaser?

And her wrist was hurting, she noticed, carefully rubbing the place where Anton Brunel had dug into her bones. Someone offered her a glass of champagne. She smiled as she took it, and hoped the thoughtful person could not see the strain in her eyes.

She did not want to be a man-teaser. She did not like what it meant.

She thought about taking a sip from her glass but she knew she would not be able to swallow. Her throat felt thick and her nerves were still jangling like mad. It was dark outside now and the air was cooler than it had been earlier. Soft lighting had been switched on to light the way to the marquee set up in the garden and the pool glittered a soft aqua blue.

She caught the smooth deep tones of Nikos's voice and turned to watch him appear in the doorway leading back into the main reception room. He was flanked either side by Santino

D'Lassio and Nina, his beautiful flame-haired wife. All three of them were smiling, relaxed— friends by their easy manner with one another.

Someone called out, 'Hey, Nina! When are you going to feed us?'

And Nina D'Lassio's light laughter filled the terrace, making Mia find a small smile too because the laughter was contagious. Then a hand arrived in the centre of her back and pushed, propelling her forward. For a moment she teetered like a ballerina on the tips of her toes, fighting the momentum trying to pitch her forwards, her eyes wide as she stared into the lit blue depths of the swimming pool.

Then she lost the battle and the next thing she knew she was falling, her sharp cry of shock the last thing she remembered before she sank beneath the depths of the cool blue waters.

Nikos was grabbing her arms even as she broke through the surface again, winded and gasping for breath. It was his fiercely clenched face she first focused on, his blazing black eyes, as he hauled her up and out of the water like a quivering, shivering, dripping wet rag.

Camera bulbs flashed in the stunning silence that hung over the pool terrace. Still too shocked to care right now, her fingers clutched at the bunched muscles in Nikos's forearms in an effort to remain standing upright. Her legs had turned to jelly and she'd lost her shoes in the tumble. Her hair had come loose and now it was dripping all over her face, and stinging hot tears were hurting her eyes.

'What happened?' Nikos roughed out harshly.

'I would swear someone gave her a push,' a disembodied voice claimed, and hearing someone say it out loud like that sent the air choking from her lungs on a broken sob.

Cursing softly Nikos tried to fold her into the shelter of his arms but she held back. 'I will wet you.'

'Do you think I care about that?'

A large warm towel arrived around her shoulders and she huddled into it gratefully, shivering badly now as the cool evening air struck deep into her wet skin.

'Are you all right, Mia—?' It was only when she heard Nina D'Lassio's anxious question that she realised it must be her hostess who'd been so quick to produce the towel she was huddling into. 'Are you hurt anywhere?'

With a shake of her head Mia made an effort to pull herself together, found the strength to push her wet hair from her face and discovered that her wrist was still hurting.

'I'm OK,' she shivered out, fighting to slow the pounding pump of her heartbeat. She managed to let out a small shrill laugh. 'I don't know how that h-happened but I will not be offended if you believe I am drunk!'

An appreciative ripple of laughter ran around the terrace. After that, people began to relax and talk again, giving her a chance to try and take stock of what she must look like. Staring down she saw that her dress was ruined, her bare toes curling into the cold white tiling in between the solid plant of Nikos's black shoes.

'Let me take care of her, Nikos,' their hostess said quietly. 'She needs to get out of those wet clothes.'

It was only then that Mia became aware of the way he was still holding her and of the fierce tension gripping him. Lifting her face up to look at him she discovered that without her shoes she had a long way to look up. Tall, dark, heart-shakingly gorgeous, it was like looking at the gladiator she'd first seen on the driveway of Balfour Manor, the flashing eyes, the fiercely clenched angular jaw, the tightly flattened mouth.

Feeling her looking at him, his black eye-lashes flickering, he tilted his dark head to look down at her with a simmering shot of barely suppressed fury that made her suck in an un-steady breath.

'I'm—OK,' she said again, feeling the

strangest need to reassure him. 'It was just such a sh-shock to hit the water like that.'

'Were you pushed?' Quiet though his voice sounded Mia still recognised the danger it attempted to suppress.

A careful glance to her left and to her right told her that some people were still standing around staring at them. The odd flashbulb reminded her that the whole incident had probably been caught on camera a hundred times over. Nina and Santino D'Lassio stood close by, and like Nikos they too were waiting to hear her response.

Moistening her trembling lips, she lowered her eyes while she tried to decide how to answer. Did she lie and say she did not know how it happened, or did she tell the truth and admit she suspected that Anton Brunel had pushed her into the pool?

'Perhaps I slipped.' She went for the least sensational option, then frowned in confusion as Nikos increased the tension in the grip he still held her in.

'Come on, Mia.' Nina D'Lassio sounded relieved though, as her arm came to rest across her shivering shoulders. 'Let's get you dry and find you something to wear…'

'I'll call for the helicopter,' Nikos said.

'No, you will not!' Mia reacted hotly. 'I have

no wish for people to think that I am a wimp as
well as Oscar's guilty mistake! *Madre di Dio*,'
she breathed fiercely, unaware that their host
and hostess were staring in surprise at her hot,
hushed flare of temper. 'I am wet and bedraggled and I saw the camera bulbs flashing. Tomorrow I will be plastered all over the papers
looking like this, and you wish to turn me into
a bigger joke by hauling me away?'

'Santino will deal with the press, Mia,' Nina
assured her quickly. 'Oh, do let go of her,
Nikos, she is not going to fall apart if you do!'

The fact that both Mia and Nina had snapped
at him seemed to wake Nikos up from wherever
he had gone off to since he'd pulled her out of
the pool. With a final flexing of impressive
clenched muscles he dropped his arms away and
took a step back, allowing Nina to lead her away.

'My security people are checking film
footage to find out what happened,' Santino
D'Lassio informed him quietly. 'Fortunately
we have a five-minute delay on what's transmitted on television, so the incident will not go up
on the screens.'

'So you think she was pushed,' Nikos said
grimly.

'You saw the way she went in there, Nikos,'
Santino responded. 'She either jumped or she
was pushed. Which do you think it was?'

Santino moved away, then began ushering his guests down to the marquee, leaving Nikos to mull over his sardonic question with his angry eyes shuttered while he replayed the moment in his head. The crush around the pool had been heavy but he'd picked Mia out of the crowd the moment he stepped outside. She'd been looking at him; he could see the way her anxious blue eyes lit up the moment they connected with his. He could *feel* them doing it, followed by the sudden jerk of her body and the look of horror and shock before she began to topple over into the pool.

What he could not see was who had been standing close enough to her to propel her into the damn pool because his full attention had been fixed exclusively on her.

'So the cuckoo almost drowned and I missed it,' a disappointed voice drawled beside him. 'What a shame.'

In no mood for Diana's Fischer's twisted kind of humour Nikos intoned flatly, 'You lead a sad life, Diana,' then walked away, over to the almost deserted pool bar and ordered a drink while he awaited Mia's return.

By the time the two women walked out of the house again he was the only person left on the terrace. As a foil for each other Mia's darkness next to Nina's flame was pretty much as good as it could get, Nikos observed. Then his full attention had welded on Mia's transformation from wet and bedraggled to long and curvaceous, a seriously slinky siren which almost blew his edgy control to bits.

She was wearing a figure-hugging strapless black tube of a dress that was nothing short of mind-stopping. For a few seconds he was thrown back to the moment he'd first seen her on the Balfour Manor driveway.

Heat poured into his body. Desire so fierce he did not know how he kept it from showing on his face. Her wet hair had been slicked back and her makeup barely there except for a fresh touch of gloss to her soft full mouth. Her natural beauty just shone out of her, warm, dark—exotic—exquisite.

But as they came closer he saw she looked deathly pale and he knew somehow—instinct—that she was more shaken up by the incident than she was trying to let on. Then he noticed the way she was holding her right wrist in the palm of her other hand and his raging libido altered to raging anger that stung like a blister trying to burn a hole in his gut.

Mia was responding with a smile to something Nina was saying when she saw Nikos slowly straighten his leaning posture from the bar. Her footsteps faltered and her eyes just clung.

'See, delivered back to you all in one piece,' Nina said teasingly. 'All you have to do, Nikos, is stop glaring like an angry bear and perhaps we can join the others and get something to eat!'

And he was glaring, Mia noticed—glaring directly at her! If he said one small word, offered up one single criticism about how she looked, she thought fiercely, then *he* would be the next one to land in the pool!

'Why are you holding your wrist like that—?' he launched at her.

CHAPTER SEVEN

GLANCING down, Mia was surprised to discover that she was indeed cupping her wrist in the palm of her other hand, 'I—I think I hurt it as I fell into the water,' she lied.

Nina let out a surprised gasp. 'Why didn't you say something?'

'Too many other things to think about,' Mia said ruefully. 'And it does not hurt as much as I am obviously making it look!'

She dropped the wrist to her side to prove her claim. Nina did not look convinced and neither did Nikos. He was still glowering at her, the tension in his jaw enough to crush rocks in his teeth. Mia frowned at him, transmitting a message that had his lush black eyelashes veiling his anger and his lips pressing together over whatever he had been about to say.

'I'm starving,' Mia said brightly in an attempt to divert attention. In truth she knew she was going to struggle to eat a single thing, and her wrist was really throbbing where it hung limp fingered at her side.

The three of them walked together down the path and into the marquee. People clapped when they saw them arrive, making Mia blush as she offered up a shy smile.

A quick murmured thanks to her hostess and Nina was rushing off to join her husband. Nikos's hand arriving against her lower back made her arch it slightly at the electric shock contact. If he noticed her reaction he said nothing, guiding her between a series of large round tables towards their allotted table. And he maintained that disturbing contact with her back right up until he had seen her into her seat.

Tension zipped back and forth between them, though Mia did not quite follow why it did. Whatever the reason, it made her respond over-brightly to the curiosity and interest which flipped backwards and forwards across the table because people were eager to know what had happened to her. She made light of their questions while Nikos lounged in the chair beside her with a polite smile strapped to his lips and his dark eyes hidden beneath his lowered eyelids.

When she could not contain a wince as she picked up her wine glass he did not know how he stopped himself from reaching out and taking the glass from her. A curse rattled around inside him because he recognised that his self-control where she was concerned was on a hair trigger. He wanted to catch hold of her injured wrist so he could inspect the damage. He wanted to brush that stray lock of damp hair from her pale cheek. He remembered what she'd said about him always touching her and the stinging tension of grim acceptance to that charge held him trapped like a prisoner, because he was becoming more and more aware of just how much and how often he wanted to touch her.

Giving his restless fingers something to do he picked up his own glass and gulped down a large slug of the rich ruby wine. She was driving him to drink, he mused bleakly.

She was driving him to many places, he extended on that, not even hearing that someone had just spoken to him. It was Mia who brought his attention back to where it should be by lightly touching his jacket sleeve. A tight sting of awareness shot up his arm and, lifting his eyelids, he looked directly into her eyes. For a second—a finely split millisecond—he visualised leaning forward to lay claim to her mouth with a soft, hot kiss.

Her eyelashes trembled and she looked away from him. She knew what he had been thinking, and the tension inside him mushroomed while he forced himself to take note of the people sharing their table. Forced himself to join in.

She was playing this out a hell of a lot better than he was, he conceded as the infernal meal dragged on and on. She only picked at the dishes set in front of her. So did he. Eventually Santino stood to give a witty speech of thanks to everyone for attending, but Nikos found it difficult to raise a smile.

And he watched Mia dip her head a little, exposing the vulnerable length of her slender nape. Tension gripped him, sexual tension. When she lifted a hand to rub at her brow, he watched her fingers tremble, saw as she lowered the hand again that her pallor seemed ten times more pronounced.

And he'd had enough. The decision came to him that quickly. People were starting to stand and move around the room now, so he used the moment to rise to his feet.

Mia was startled when he cupped her elbow and drew her to her feet but she did not protest when he just turned with her and headed out of the marquee without saying a word to anyone. There was a charity auction to follow the banquet, then music and dancing and a cabaret show put on by attending celebrities, which was to be transmitted to the Lake Como party by satellite link.

He did not seem to give a damn. He ignored the clicking rush of camera shutters and the TV cameras recording their departure, his long loose stride tempered to suit her smaller steps in Nina's borrowed shoes, and his hand was in possession of the curving indent of her waist.

They walked the path up to the house in taut trammelling silence. As they passed by the pool Mia could not control a small shiver and he reacted to it by drawing her in closer to his side. He was using his mobile to speak to his pilot as they stepped into the house. By the time they stepped out of it again by the front door she could see the helicopter coming in to settle on the same patch of lawn it had dropped them off on when they arrived.

A few minutes later and she subsided gratefully into her seat. Her wrist was aching and a tension headache was tugging at the backs of her eyes.

'OK,' he said the moment they were airborne. 'Tell me what happened.'

Casting a glance in his direction, Mia saw that his mood did not look good at all. He was sitting with his long legs stretched out in front of him and a black-suited elbow rested on the window's narrow ledge. A set of long fingers supported the golden jut of his jaw while one finger lay across the thin stretch of his mouth.

And his dark eyes glittered.

'I don't know what happened,' she answered, keeping to her decision to play the whole incident down.

'If you're lying to me I will find out,' he warned her quietly. 'Santino's staff is checking film footage as we speak. I saw you fall, and I believe you were pushed. I want to know who you think did that to you and *why* you believe that they did.'

'It could just have been an accident,' Mia sighed out. 'I don't understand why you are obsessing on it.'

For an answer he dipped his hand into his pocket and drew out his mobile. She knew without having to ask that he was going to call Santino and get the information he wanted from him.

'You are such a bully—put your phone away,' she snapped, adding another sigh of weary surrender this time when he continued to hold the phone at the ready, eyes fixed like stubborn black lasers on her pale face.

'I think it was Anton Brunel that pushed me,' she admitted.

'Brunel?' Nikos fired a sharp frown at her. 'He was there tonight?'

Moistening her taut lips Mia nodded. 'He—approached me as I was about to go outside…' Her eyes darkened with anger when she recalled the way he had grabbed her and hustled her into that corner. 'He caught hold of me and began throwing all kinds of wild accusations at me. He—he claimed I had lied to you. That I had been flirting with him.' She just could not bring herself to use Anton Brunel's shameful term.

'And were you—flirting with him?'

'How dare you say that? How dare you *ask* me that?' Mia turned on him furiously. 'We have had this conversation before and I was not pleased with your attitude then!' she heaved out in an offended rush.

'You used him to pull my strings with that dossier and your description of what happened between the two of you that day.' Nikos tossed out a broad-shouldered shrug. 'How do I know you did not start your string-pulling campaign with a bit of flirtation across the lunch table with him?'

'So I am a dreadful flirt and a cunning manipulator—is that what you're saying?' Mia was stunned by the level of *both* men's conceit! But most of all she was horrified that they might be right! 'I suppose you also think I deserved all I got when I landed in the pool!'

'I didn't say that.'

'But you implied it!' So upset now, she pushed up her chin and looked away from him, fighting the tears trying to burn in her eyes. 'He bruised my wrist too but I suppose I should apologise for not allowing him to throttle me at the same time!' she shook out thickly. 'Perhaps you could— W-what are you doing—?' she broke off to choke out.

He'd undone his seat belt and arrived across the gap separating them with the speed of an attacking snake! Now he was picking up her bruised wrist and inspecting it, the curses that flooded from him in several different languages should have turned the dark night air bright blue.

'I will kill him,' he rasped, going pale with fury when he saw the livid purple fingerprints marking her delicate skin.

Mia snatched her wrist back, hurting it in the bargain, but she just did not care. 'You...men— you are all the same, ready to parade your macho strength when you feel like it,' she shook out in burning contempt. 'Yet you are quick to play the victims when a woman so much as looks at you! No, don't touch me.' She jerked away when he tried to capture her bruised wrist again. 'I am angry with you!'

'I can see that,' Nikos said quietly.

Her face flushed, the tears daring to press against the muscles in her throat now. 'I be-haved myself tonight—for your benefit! I did not do anything to earn your contempt! It was not my f-fault that a nasty p-person like Anton Brunel wished to push me in the pool—and you are not my hero just because you happened to pull me out of it!'

The helicopter had come to a standstill without either of them noticing. Mia undid her seat belt and stepped over Nikos, just needing to get out of there before she did something really stupid like bursting into a flood of hot tears!

She was already halfway to the house by the time Nikos had stepped onto the darkened lawn. With a growl of frustration he strode after her and entered the house in time to watch her fly up the stairs. And even in flight the sensual flow of her lush black-clad figure reacted on him with all the gut-grinding promise of a—

'*Theos,*' he breathed.

He wanted her.

His hand snaked up to grab hold of the back of his neck.

He was not her hero, but he had this angry desire to charge up those damn stairs after her and at least be her lover!

He remained standing like that for the next thirty control-clutching seconds—until he heard her bedroom door close with a thud. Then with a violent swing of his body he strode off towards the back of the house, discarding his clothes as he went. By the time he reached the door which led into his all-purpose gym he was almost naked but for a pair of black cotton undergarments that moulded his fiercest problem with no conscience at all.

He used the gym as if it was his own personal war zone, pounding his body through a series of physical drills that did nothing to ease what was really driving him. Giving up on that form of torture he slammed through another door and dived into the glistening blue waters of his indoor swimming pool. Fifty hard laps later and he was climbing out again and heading back through the house, grimly gathering up his discarded clothes as he went.

The moment he reached his bedroom he headed for the bathroom. The heat of the shower made his glistening skin sweat and his chest was heaving from his recent exertions, but one part of him still dominated everything else. Cursing he switched the shower to cold and punished himself by letting the icy water dowse his entire frame. By the time he came out of the bathroom covered by a white towelling robe he thought he was finally beginning to get a grip.

Then a soft knock sounded on his bedroom door and he knew, even as he walked barefoot across the room, that no matter how hard he'd worked at it, he'd controlled nothing at all. For there was only one person in this house who could be knocking on his door and she was naive enough and blind enough not to know what she was tempting by doing it.

And there she stood in a short ivory silk robe with her recently shampooed hair a pagan swathe of glossy damp waves around her beautiful face. Her blue eyes looked anxious. A set of even white teeth were pressing into her full bottom lip.

'I'm s-sorry to disturb you,' she stammered out, 'but I n-need…'

The stammer did it; the big blue eyes staring up at him did it, the pearly white teeth worrying her lip. She'd been disturbing him for too many frustrating hours and days and weeks, and he just reached for her and pulled her into his arms, then drove his hungry mouth down onto hers.

And the hell of it was, she let him. Next thing he knew he was stepping back with her trapped against him and kicking the door shut so he could press her back against it to indulge in the kind of hot sensual embrace that said goodbye to his self-control.

Mia fell into the kiss like a starving woman. It was so much what she wanted there wasn't a single second when she thought to pull free. Her arms had already wrapped around his neck to fasten tightly and she was kissing him back so deep and hotly she did not recognise herself. The feel of his strong hard masculine body pressing against her felt glorious, the flood tide of pleasure that went rushing through her made her gasp and groan and quiver feverishly as he explored her mouth with a deep hot knowing intimacy which had her lips open wider in search for more.

Her reward was a lusty masculine growl that excited her dreadfully. Tightening his arms around her he lifted her up against him and fed her legs around his waist, then just stood there with her clamped against him, their parted mouths fused together and the intimacy taking place with their tongues a shattering mimic of something else he was doing to her.

His hands were splayed across her silk-covered buttocks, the fiercely bold evidence of how he was feeling shocked and excited her in equal amounts. When she moved voluptuously against him she felt his shudder that blew the last of his common sense to bits.

Turning to walk with her over to the bed, as they landed on the mattress in a tangle of clinging limbs, he pulled his head back. 'What did you come here for?' he rasped out.

Having to fight to try and understand the question, Mia opened her eyes and just stared blankly up at him. His mouth was barely an inch away, his warm breath scoring her face. She could feel the pounding pump of his heart against her tightening breasts as he waited for her to give him a response. To tell him she had come here to ask for a couple of headache pills was just not going to leave her warm moist swollen tongue. This was more important. She no longer even had a headache!

When she didn't say anything, with a softly grated curse he repeated the question, watched her blink slowly, watched her teeth press down into that hot plump lower lip—and lost patience.

'Well, I'm in no mood to stop now,' he groaned thickly. 'So if you decide that you do want to stop you're going to have to say it loud and clear.'

But Mia did not want to stop. And she proved it by running her fingers into his thick black wet silken curls on his head and drew his mouth back to hers. She could not explain it, did not want to try and explain it. All she knew was that, tough as he was, and hard and cold and dangerous as he was, Nikos Theakis had grabbed something from her that day on Oscar's driveway and deposited this terrible need for more of him in its place.

The kiss drove out any need for more talking;

it was hungry and it was deep. And he was so practiced at this she barely felt his weight on top of her or the deft way that he undid her robe belt. The burning pleasure when she felt their naked bodies come together was just about the most overwhelming sensation she had ever felt.

He knew what he was doing, so she just hung on and followed where he led, revelling in each new and exciting experience. He knew just where to touch her, knew just when to break their mouths apart so he could drive her frantic with slow moist kisses down the length of her body. He splayed long fingers around one firm tender breast and teased its shy sensitive bud to flower and tighten, then caught his prize in his mouth.

Wild pleasure took her over, her body arching and her thighs trembling as she gasped out his name. His fingers stroked her ribcage, trailing a path of fire down to her stomach and, finally, shocking her into complete stillness when he made that first sweep between the thighs.

Her breathless stillness brought his head up, eyes drugged and blackened by passion honing on to her face. Her hair flowed across the pillow; her hands still held his head. Her eyes were closed, her soft lips parted, and she was quivering—flesh, muscles, bones all vibrating in unison at the first exploratory caress he made. She did not seem to have any control over what she was feeling. Control, Nikos realised, belonged exclusively to him.

When her restless fingers trailed his nape, then slithered down his burning chest, he groaned as his body responded violently.

She shaped the bunched muscles in his wide shoulders as her slender hips arched into his. She held nothing back, and he felt so intoxicated by her he sunk them both down—down into the dark heat of passion until it was all she could do to cling to him and let him dictate the rest.

It was like being lost, floating on a rocky sea of building pleasure, Mia likened hazily. When he reared back from her to remove his towel, her heavy eyes drank in the powerful beauty of his body—coveted it, reached out and touched the whirl of dark hair between his bulging pectoral muscles and made him shudder as she scored him with her fingernails.

He came back to her on a hiss of hunger, lay over her, letting her feel the glorious heat of his naked flesh against her own once again. It was power versus weakness, hard versus soft. He nibbled at the corner of her mouth until she twisted her head and anxiously demanded the full onslaught of his mouth.

Passion, desire, overrode everything. He made love to her slowly and erotically and intensely, his sensual caresses moving her closer and closer to a place she had never been before. Her fingers plucked restlessly at his flesh, her teeth fastened on to his throat. He was hot, a film of salty male sweat tasting on her tongue. She could not keep still and she could feel the tense state of his erection pushing against her thigh.

'Nikos,' she whimpered over and over for some dizzyingly important reason she could not understand.

He understood though.

She felt her first spark of self-consciousness when she suddenly remembered that she was nothing like the long slender blondes he was used to looking at like this. She had curves. She had a waist and hips and full real breasts, not fakes. As if he was thinking along similar lines an odd twist of a smile curved his lips as his gaze flickered down to that other difference she was suddenly acutely aware of, the triangle of ebony curls nestling at the juncture with her thighs.

Then he bent down and kissed her navel; it was so shockingly unexpected, her muscles jerked violently in response. One of his hands stretched out, grabbing hold of her hand as it went instinctively to push him away from her, long fingers closing around her fingers as he repeated the kiss with a slow and sensual glide of his tongue lower and lower.

'Nikos, no,' she groaned out.

He ignored her protest and was so ruthless about his intentions that she surrendered to the silky waves of pleasure he was making her feel, her eyelids folding downwards as he traced each moist, hot, swollen part of her. Within seconds he was carrying her way beyond sense, drugging her with the newness of one sensation laid on top of another. The way he used his tongue to pleasure her, the way he continued to clasp her hand. The way her limbs had gone boneless and restless, the way there was a slow languorous drag of her breathing. He knew exactly what he was doing to her as he moved up her body to the flat of her stomach, the curve of her ribs, the tight tender peaks of her breasts and finally, with a hungry moulding of his lips, to her mouth.

And with a single lithe move he arrived on top of her, his narrow hips pressing between her trembling thighs and at last she experienced the sense-spinning intimacy of his bold erection sliding into her like hot smooth silk.

'*Madre di Dio,*' she breathed, '*non posso più,*' as she shot right over the pleasure threshold.

And still he held one of her hands captive, still he ravaged her mouth. She was wild, she was scared, she could not keep her legs still. Her free hand was clawing at his bronzed damp flesh, the breath leaving her in short tense little bursts. Pleasure was lighting her up from the inside, bright hot shimmering pleasure she had no control over as it built and built. And he was hot—burning, murmuring things to her she could not understand, though some instinct inside her recognised that he was urging her on and on.

'*Non posso più*,' she whispered a second time.

'*Sì*, you can stand it,' he responded thickly. 'Hold on to me, Mia. There's a lot more to come.'

And he was right, there was so much more of it and on so many levels she just couldn't keep up. Her dizzy world went misty, she was held enthralled by how acutely she could feel every centimetre of him as he slowly filled her up.

He was hot and trembling, so lost in the sheer power of what he was generating between them he forgot just what kind of creature it was he was holding in his arms. He was only aware of the desire, the hunger, the passion, raging through both of them. He felt it, fed it and eventually surrendered to it, and with a heavy groan drove home with a final deep stabbing thrust.

Mia had forgotten to expect it. So the sharp spasm of pain locked her muscles in shock. She could not breathe, she could not think. Nikos had frozen on top of her, his eyes like black caverns blazing down into her stark staring blue eyes already swimming with tears.

He started cursing and she started sobbing, hitting out at him with her tightly clenched fists. He eased back a little, cursing all over again, his eyes closing as her tense muscles unwittingly clung to him sending waves of pleasure rippling his powerful frame.

'It's OK.' He tried to look for sanity, his hands gently capturing her two clenched fists. 'It's OK, *agape mou*,' he repeated, though he knew nothing had ever been less OK, because he was already hungrily moulding her lips to his. He managed to hold the pressure back. He managed to control his rampant needy senses long enough to give her chance to adjust.

And she felt wonderful, narrow and tight and so deliciously hot. His breathing was hectic, hers was the same, the two of them fighting for breath in panting urgency around the clinging darting heat of the tongue. He felt her clenched fists relax their tension, then her taut slender body slowly ease from its crucifying arch. Their hearts were beating like crazy hammers, sending tremor after tremor rippling across their flesh. Slowly, carefully, he released her fingers and groaned in relief when she instantly ran them into his hair. He fed his hands beneath her to support her and with the flickering passion of his tongue against her tongue, he just lost it altogether and let his hips surge forward, thrusting him deep.

It was as if a whole tidal wave of pleasure rushed through her, hot as lava and sweet as melting honey. Caught in its thrall Mia raised her hips to take him in farther and sent a thick moaning cry into his mouth. Dragging her pulsing lips free she whispered, 'Again,' and felt him draw back, then thrust again. It was the sweet—sweet—sweetest torment. 'Oh, again,' she gasped out.

Feeling drunk on her greedy pleasure, Nikos caught her mouth and ravished its soft swollen fullness and set the deep and fluid motion of loving with a rampant erotic thoroughness that emptied his head of all else but her and this and what he could feel was building between them. Never in his long sexual experience had he ever felt anything so intensely as this. She moved with him with an innate sensuality born of instinct. She clung to him with her arms and her legs. When the final madness began to accelerate them towards their climaxes, he could feel that she was with him every blindingly glorious step of the way.

And it went on and on, like time never ending. Mouths separate now, Mia felt every single sense she possessed sing to a pleasure that just grew and grew.

'Nikos,' she whispered, floating up her heavy eyelids to look at him. Her eyes clung to his eyes where the sheer power of his feelings burned, naked and exposed. The first jolt of blinding pleasure brought forth a sharp cry from her throat, followed by another one, and he plunged deeper, catching her up to him in his strong arms and holding her, the rasping race of his breathing something she only understood when he joined her in the exquisite pleasure of hot drowning release.

Afterwards was almost as good as the climax to this first loving Mia had ever experienced. The slow sensual reactionary quivers that brought her downwards slowly, the awareness of his hot skin against hers. The size and weight of him, the strength and the power of his wonderful masculine magnificence crushing her down into the bed.

And the way he still held her, close, so close. *'Bello—bello,'* she breathed on a fragile wisp of a murmur.

Easing her of his weight, Nikos slid onto

his side, taking her with him. Content to remain lost in the hazy aftermath of sweet pleasure, it was all she could do to curl against the man who had just made her first experience so wildly beautiful and gloriously passionate.

While Mia floated, Nikos felt as if he'd just come down to earth with a thud after enjoying one of the most exciting releases of his life. Payback, he named it, staring over the top of her tumbled raven locks into the stark face of what he had just done.

He had just broken his own cardinal rule and taken an innocent, and what's more she was a Balfour innocent. He could already hear the wedding bells ringing, could feel the noose closing around his throat. As the chilling face of reality spread its icy fingers out across his flesh he sensed her drifting into sleep. She was curled lovingly against him, warm and soft and so damn trusting with her cheek resting against the unsteady thump of his heartbeat and her fingers gently stroking the whorls of damp dark hair on his chest.

But she didn't know him. Even Oscar, who knew him better than anyone, did not know who the real Nikos Theakis was. It was safer not to know him, safer to keep himself crushed so deep inside he would never rear his head. If that meant he had to crush the more human emotions at the same time, then that was the way it had to be.

People looked at him and saw the smooth billionaire entrepreneur, ruthlessly focused on his career. They saw the cool sophisticated male who turned out for elite functions like the one they'd attended this evening, or the good-looking guy with a trail of beautiful well-satisfied women drifting behind him in his wake.

They did not know that he needed to shower four times a day—more often if he had the opportunity, or that there were no locks on any doors in any of his homes except for the locks on main entrances.

They did not know that he always—always—slept alone. That this beautiful creature sleeping curled around him now was actually receiving a twisted kind of honour, because he had not already shaken her awake and sent her packing back to her own room to sleep.

As if she could sense what he was thinking she moved against him, a soft sigh escaping her parted lips as she stretched, then relaxed again, the movement so fluid and naturally sensual Nikos had to clench his body to stop it from responding to it. One of her long silken legs lay warm across his, her fingers lay buried in the whorls of dark hair on his chest.

She murmured something—*ti'amo*, he thought she said, and felt its emotive impact like a violent crash to his chest. *Ti'amo*, I love you. *Ti'amo*, I so belong to you now it's a done deal, he translated with harsh mocking bitterness.

And like a man making a dangerous bid for escape, he eased himself free of her clinging shape and gave her a pillow to hug instead of him. She curled around it like some beautiful dark sensual siren clinging on to her latest victim, and with no idea that the cold ruthless side to his nature was busily rearing its awesome head.

CHAPTER EIGHT

A SOUND awoke Mia as the quiet light of dawn was drifting in through the window. She continued to lie there for a few seconds, grappling to make sense of her unfamiliar surroundings, then she remembered and her heart gave a thump. Twisting her head on the pillow she saw that the place beside her in the bed was empty, and she sat up with a jerk, a hand going up to push her tumbled hair from her face. The sound came again and she focused on Nikos, who was standing with his back to her on the other side of the room.

He was already dressed in one of the dark business suits he favoured, and was snapping his paper-thin watch to his wrist. He looked so breathtakingly handsome that tender muscles deep in her abdomen responded with a pulse of awareness at the same moment she picked up the clean male scents permeating the room which told her he had recently showered.

The sheer novel intimacy in their situation suddenly engulfed her in a rosy hue of shyness. Realising she was also very naked beneath the thin sheet had her clutching at its fine linen edge and drawing it up to her chin before she could fight a drowning wash of self-consciousness to speak.

'What—what time is it?' she asked huskily.

The way his wide shoulders tensed at the sound of her voice sent her teeth biting down into her soft lower lip. Perhaps he was not quite comfortable with their new situation yet either, she allowed.

'Five o'clock,' he answered without turning. 'Go back to sleep—it's too early for you to get up.'

'You are up,' Mia pointed out to him.

He said nothing, his long fingers reaching out to pick up his mobile phone, which he placed in his jacket pocket, followed by some other bits and pieces Mia followed without really registering what they were. Beginning to frown now, it was slowly dawning on her that he did not want to look at her. That the tension gripping his wide shoulders also repeated itself in the sharp movements of his fingers, and from the small amount of his profile she could see, the muscle that angled his strong jaw was clenched.

'I am about to leave,' he announced suddenly,

making Mia blink slowly. 'I have business to attend to in Rome. My plane is on standby. Enjoy the rest of your day here if you wish. When you are ready to go back to London, let Lukas know and he will have my helicopter come and collect you.'

Every word, every cool flat businesslike word, arriving like the cold tip of a knife's blade forced Mia to recognise what he was doing. He had taken her to his bed; now he was distancing himself. In true Nikos Theakis tried-and-tested tradition he was letting her know without needing to say the words that this—this soulless departure in the pale hours of the morning marked the end of what they had shared!

Beginning to tremble, Mia shut her eyes, struggling with a nauseating sense of hurt that made her burst forth with the shaken words, 'Don't do this to me, Nikos.'

He moved, twisting the long length of his body to lance her a brief shuttered glance. 'Don't beg, Mia. It's unbecoming.'

Beg—? Her eyes flicked open in time to watch him turn away again, every lean hard elegant inch of him so contained she began to feel dizzy now as well as sick.

'I am not begging,' she denied on a wounded choke. 'We—we just slept together!'

'A—mistake. It should not have happened.'

'But it *did* happen.'

'True.' He seemed to be inordinately interested in what was inside his wallet now. 'However, it will not be happening again.'

'Just like that?' Beginning to squirm with self-loathing for even trying to discuss this with him, Mia folded her arms around her knees and crushed them to her chest. 'You—you make love to me, then just—just throw me aside as if my feelings do not count?'

'*Theos!* We did not make love, we had sex!' He spun on her angrily. 'We had wild hot amazing sex—Mia!' he repeated harshly. 'Where was the love in what we did in that bed last night? I did not bring it there! And if you did, then you were—'

His nostrils flared as he snapped his lips together, drawing back from what he had been about to say next. His dark eyes blazed at her frozen expression of horror, then with a muttered curse he turned his back to her again.

'I was w-what?' she prompted sickly, feeling like someone living a nightmare she could not wake up from. She found she could not let him stop there even if the rest was going to break her in two. 'Naive? Stupid? Ready for it? *Begging* you for it?'

His lean profile clenched. 'I was not going to say any of that.'

'Then what were you going to say!' she
fired out.

'Nothing.'

The liar, the cruel wicked liar!

'I hate you so much now I will never forgive you for doing this to me,' she whispered.
'No doubt you are relieved and pleased to
hear me say it!'

'Actually, I'm not—' his voice remained cool
'—I…care about you, Mia. But I'm a loner. I
always have been. I don't do the kind of relationship you are going to expect. You will not
believe this right now but I'm doing you a big
favour calling a halt now—'

'As you do with all the other women who
have shared this bed with you?' she flung out.
'Take w-what you want from them, then toss
them to one side like yesterday's rubbish?'

'Exactly like that,' he confirmed.

Stunned that he had dared to admit it as
coolly at he had, Mia stared at him for a second,
then pushed her face into her knees and hugged
self-loathing to her like it was her closest friend.
She'd never felt so cheap, so used and discarded. And whatever it was he had tried *not* to
say, the real truth crucifying her right now was
she *had* been asking for it—*begging* him for
it—for weeks before he gave in!

Now here she sat in the middle of his

rumpled bed consigned to the low ranks of a one-night stand.

Which was probably her just deserts for being such an easy tramp!

'Why don't you just go,' she whispered when she sensed him still hovering.

'I…need to know you are going to be all right.'

So he wanted reassurance now? 'I'm all right.' She gave it to him with the taste of bitterness in her mouth.

And still he hovered! Why—? Was he going to ask for a litre or two of her blood next?

'Look…' he said heavily. 'I'm—sorry I let this happen.' He actually sounded it too. 'It was all my fault. I should not have given in to what was happening between us. You're young and inexperienced in these things but I am not, and I should have…'

'Say anything else m-more disgusting to me and I will be sick!' Mia wrenched out.

'It was wrong!' he lashed out suddenly. 'I dishonoured you and I dishonoured your father—'

That brought her head flying upwards. 'Don't you *dare* bring Oscar into this!' she lashed back, dizzy at the unexpected hot flare of awareness she experienced when she looked at him. 'How dare you stand there and speak his name to me as if you have some right to hold him up against me!'

His taut profile paled. 'I did not mean—'

'I do not care what you did not mean! I do not care that you feel guilty now that you've had Oscar's daughter in this bed! I gave myself to you willingly and freely. It is you who finds this a shameful thing, not me!'

Standing rigid with shock, he looked as if he'd been turned into rock, and Mia decided she'd had taken enough of this. With an infuriatingly uncontrollable sob, she coiled her fingers around the sheet and snaked off the bed, dragging the sheet with her as she went.

'Mia…'

'No,' she husked out. 'Don't speak another word to me. I *hate* you. I will hate you for ever.'

Those black feelings vented, she ran into his bathroom and slammed the door shut, then just sank in a puddle of white linen to the floor.

Go away and learn to honour yourself, Oscar had said to her. Well, she had shot that ideal in the foot, for where had her sense of honour been when she had lusted after Nikos Theakis? Where was it in recognising that she had just turned into the one person she had always vowed she would never turn into—her high-class whoring mother!

And she would never forgive Nikos for

making her aware that this was what she had done to herself.

She heard the telltale sound of the helicopter lifting off the ground as she still sat in her huddle on the bathroom floor.

He'd gone. Her aching heart turned over. He had not bothered to hang around for a second longer than he absolutely had to and she hated him for doing that too.

A few minutes after she had been delivered back to her apartment via helicopter, then a chauffeured limousine, which left her feeling cynically unimpressed, Sophie called her.

'Have you seen the papers today? Someone had an interesting time last night,' she teased. 'Did you go skinny dipping in the D'Lassios' pool because you were hot?'

Mia sank into the nearest chair and closed her weary eyes. So, despite assurances from Santino, her trip into the pool had found its way into the press.

'Explain this skinny dipping,' she requested.

'Self-explicit turn of phrase,' Sophie said. 'OK, so you had all your clothes on,' she conceded, 'but the photo of the great and gorgeous Nikos hauling you out of the pool without so much as splashing himself looks impressive, while you looked kind of—wet and helpless and cute.'

Cute. Mia pressed her lips together because they wanted to tremble.

'What happened?'

'I—slipped in the crush,' she lied. 'Is there anything else in the papers I should know about?' she then asked.

'Only this amazing picture of you leaving later wearing the sexiest dress I've ever seen on you. Was it Nina's?'

'*Sì*.'

'She has fabulous taste,' Sophie gushed. 'You went from fairy princess in floating blue silk chiffon to wet and helpless to dramatically slinky all in one evening. I wish I could wear a dress like that,' she sighed out wistfully.

'You could if you only stopped trying to hide your lovely figure under metres of fabric,' Mia murmured impatiently.

'Oh, come on, Mia. I'm five foot three inches high to your five-eight,' Sophie pointed out. 'Long and slinky I am not and never will be. Besides the unplanned dip, did you enjoy the rest of the evening or did you need to take the courage pill halfway through?'

Just like that her half-sister guided the subject away from herself as she always did, Mia noticed. Then she felt her insides curl up and sink because the rest of the evening did not bear thinking about.

'The rest of the evening was—OK,' she mumbled.

'You're distinctly unimpressed, then, that Nikos spent a cool half-million at the auction on a diamond bracelet.'

He did? Mia blinked. They had left before the auction had even started! He must have placed his bid before they left, she decided, murmuring out loud and cynically, 'Perhaps he collects them to give out to his one-night stands as they leave.'

'Oh, wow,' Sophie murmured. 'Now that sounded bitter.'

Mia was glad to hear it confirmed. She hoped to build on the bitterness she felt towards Nikos Theakis until it had successfully wiped out these other feelings of hopeless, useless love and hate and hard, crushing hurt.

Pride alone made her turn in for work on Monday morning to find herself the sinecure for a battery of wary glances and terribly reserved smiles. It was only then that she remembered the bruising kiss in a sunny car park which she discovered was now the property of every employer in the building and had effectively wiped out all the natural friendliness she had been gifted with in the preceding weeks.

'What did you expect?' Fiona asked her. 'You can't indulge in a relationship with the boss and expect everyone to continue to treat you like one of them. You're a Balfour. He's a billionaire. You've confirmed their original expectations of you and now they feel duped.'

What could she say in her own defence? That the kiss had been a form of punishment because she'd likened him to a donkey called Tulio? Or that he'd used the kiss to warn off the guy from accounts because Nikos believed he'd stood her up on a date? The first was really stupid and unbelievable in the cold light of a new day. And the second excuse exposed her own lie to Nikos in the first place.

By the end of the week she'd closed herself off inside a steel case of protection so that nothing else could threaten her very shaky composure. Nikos had not returned to London and she had stopped eating. In truth she felt too wounded and raw to eat. Fiona was constantly sending her worried glances. Even her aunt noticed the difference in her voice when they talked on the phone.

'Is something wrong, Mia?' she asked her.

'I'm missing you,' she said, and it was the truth. She was missing *Tia* and Tuscany, and the quiet calm simplicity of the life she'd led there.

'But otherwise you are happy with your exciting new life?'

Tia Giulia wanted her to say yes. She needed

to be reassured that she had not made a big mistake telling Mia about Oscar. So Mia gave her that assurance and tried after that to sound much brighter when she phoned.

On Saturday, she bumped into one of Kat Balfour's friends in the street. Bethany was a bright, beautiful, lively creature much like her half-sister Kat. They chatted about the D'Lassio party for a while, which Bethany had been unable to attend for some reason Mia could not recall two minutes after she'd had it explained to her. Her mind was like that right now, unable to sustain any thoughts that did not contain the name Nikos Theakis in them. Bethany invited her to join her and a few other friends for a drink that night and Mia thought emptily, why not?

When she arrived at the Chelsea wine bar the place was so crowded she almost chickened out and went away again, but Bethany saw her and waved her over. Bathany's group of friends were lively and noisy and Mia was surprised an hour later to discover that she was almost— almost—enjoying herself. Most of them were going on to dinner, then a nightclub, but the thought of eating anything made her stomach go queasy so she declined with a smile and some excuse that was something else she could not recall minutes afterwards.

The following Wednesday, she climbed out of bed and immediately had to run to the bathroom where she was sick. When the same thing happened the next few mornings, she decided it was time to start eating proper, regular meals again.

Monday, she still felt so nauseous Fiona noticed her sickly pallor.

'I think I've caught a bug,' she confessed and explained that she'd been sick on and off for days.

Fiona sent her home. Not wanting to go because being stuck in her apartment all day was only marginally worse than being stuck here waiting for Nikos to put in an appearance. He called daily but he only spoke to Fiona. In the time he had been away he'd called from Rome, Athens, New York and Busan. Understanding just where Busan was put him a long, long way away, which suited her, Mia told herself.

It *did*.

Wednesday, Fiona showed her an article from the financial pages of a broadsheet. It was about Lassiter-Brunel. Apparently the company had a new anonymous backer to bail them out of trouble. Good, she thought. Perhaps Anton Brunel will stop being angry with her for ruining his deal with Nikos.

Thursday she stood up from her desk too

quickly and went so dizzy she almost passed out. Angry and concerned, Fiona insisted she go to see a doctor because the stomach bug was lingering too long. Having never needed to consult a doctor in her entire life before, she had no idea how to find one in London. So she had to call Sophie, who wanted to know what was wrong. After explaining, her half-sister directed her to the family physician. She took a taxi there. The moment she stepped into his private rooms, she knew she did not want to be there. Something—instinct maybe—filled her with a stark feeling of dread. Half an hour later she walked out again, so shocked and dazed she almost walked straight under the wheels of a car. She did not go back to the office. She did not go back to her apartment. She just walked and walked and walked, until eventually thirst and exhaustion forced her to hail a taxi and go home.

The mirrored walls in the lift showed her deathly colour. A trembling weakness in her legs had forced her to lean into the corner of the car.

'*Incinta…*' She watched her lips form a word that was still refusing to make proper sense to her.

She even tried mouthing the same thing in English but could not seem to remember the translation and her eyes looked like two sunken dark pools in her wan face. A fresh clutch of nausea was building, drying up her mouth and flattening her hands to her stomach in an effort to stop it from getting any worse.

The lift stopped and the doors slid open. Reeling her way out of it like a dizzy drunk she almost cannoned right into the big man himself. Dressed in a dark grey suit with a gold tie knotted against his bright white shirt, he looked staggeringly elegant, shatteringly attractive and felt so solidly real that Mia just lost it completely, and every shocked, scared, raw emotion she had been struggling with throughout the afternoon just exploded from her in a fit of helpless rage.

She hit out at him, managing to land a salvo of blows on his chest before he caught firm hold of her fists to hold them still. Stopped from venting her feelings that way and panting in her fury she went for the jugular with the only other weapon left.

'What are you doing here?' She speared up at his surprised, disgustingly healthy-looking handsome dark face. 'You should be feeling too ashamed to show your face!'

'Mia—'

'Don't you dare say my name to me!' she choked, yanking like a crazy woman at her imprisoned fists. 'You turned me into my mother and I *hate* you for it! I will hate you for doing that to me for the rest of my life!'

With a final tug he let go of her, and the moment he did so she slithered round him, too engrossed in her own raw feelings to notice that, other than capturing her fists, he had been totally still throughout her attack.

Her legs felt wobbly when she tried to walk on them; the queasy feeling in her stomach had now reached her throat. She wasn't really surprised that when she tried to focus on her apartment door, the oval-shaped walls of the lobby began to sway in and out. Reaching out for the nearest solid thing in an effort to steady herself, her trembling fingers closed around the hard-muscled strength of a silk-suited arm instead.

Mia tilted her head back, glazed blue eyes darkened by confusion staring at his fiercely frowning expression. She had not heard him move. Perhaps he had not moved at all and it was just an optical illusion like the moving walls and the swaying floor beneath her feet.

Then it all began to close in on her. 'Nikos,' she whispered just before she began to sink.

When she came around she was lying on a long soft leather sofa. Nikos was squatting down beside it, lancing Greek into his mobile phone while he held one of her hands trapped inside a tightly clenched grip.

He looked clenched all over, Mia observed dimly, gliding an unwilling glance over his taut profile and the fierce set of his shoulders inside his jacket. Nor did he look as elegantly turned out as he had done. He'd dragged the knot to his tie loose and undone two buttons of his shirt. Those two buttons looked as if they'd been yanked open to reveal a triangle of brown skin. There was tension in his strong neck muscles and his clenched jaw line. And as he bit out another line of Greek she noticed his blanched pallor and the lines of stress spoiling the shape of his wide sensual lips.

How long had she been out? Frowning, it took her several seconds to recall the full drama she had enacted before she'd swooned away at his feet. She'd attacked him like a madwoman. She had not even given him a chance to speak. She recalled his stunned frozen face when she'd vented her anger on him.

Then she remembered *why* she had reacted like that and a tiny sob escaped her lips.

His conversation stopped. He swung his dark head around to look at her. Fierce dark eyes that glittered with the oddest expression settled on hers and the fingers he had closed around her fingers tightened their grip.

'You fainted,' he told her as if she was too dense to work it out for herself.

Mia said nothing. Looking at him should be hurting by now and she was waiting for the pain to kick in.

'You are in my apartment,' he added after making a wary foray of her pale unresponsive countenance. 'I carried you in here. You—scared me.'

Scared him? He did not know the meaning of scared, Mia thought dismally. Scared was what had made her attack him the way that she did.

As he was going to find out soon enough when she broke the news to him.

If she told him.

'So I've called in a doctor.'

Mia snaked her fingers free. 'That was not necessary.'

'It was to me.'

Sitting up carefully in case she set off her fragile stomach again, she made a move with her legs that gave him no choice but to stand if he did not want her to unbalance him. Her head was still swimming and, pushing a set of fingers up to her brow, she was forced to remain sitting on his sofa when really she would have loved to just get up and walk out without speaking another word to him.

Pregnant…

At last the English translation had come to

her. For some incomprehensible reason it had more impact in English. A hard word, abrupt—pregnant—no softness or sentimentality in it at all, unlike the so-much-gentler *incinta*...

'You've lost weight.'

Lowering her hand she looked up and found he was standing several feet away, tall as a tree and blocking out most of the light from the window behind him, placing his face in shadow so she could not read his expression.

But she did not need light to feel the tension emanating from him.

'You might as well call the doctor back and tell him not to bother because I will not see him,' she said, looking away again because she could feel the first quivering beginning of hurt kicking in.

'I am not ill.' To prove it she made herself stand. 'I am simply hungry because I forgot to eat today.'

'And the day before that and the day before that,' Nikos threw in. 'There is hardly anything left of you and you are swaying where you stand. If you try to take a step you will probably hit the floor again—unless I catch you as I did before, of course, which is up for question right now because I am bloody angry with you, Mia. So angry I could give you a shake.'

'You are *angry*—with me?' Lifting up her

chin her eyes sparked incredulous blue. 'What do you think gives you the right to be *anything* where I am concerned?'

Ignoring that he said, 'I've spoken to Fiona. You have been feeling unwell all week—'

Only for a week? Mia almost laughed at the understatement.

'And you've been—going out drinking.'

Starting to wonder if she really had fainted again and not come around yet, Mia stared at his stiff censorious stance and waited to find out what her delirious imagination was going to make him say next!

'With friends of Kat's,' he provided.

'Fiona told you all of this?' Even in her imagination she could not envisage his secretary would have offered up this kind of information about her.

'No.' He made a tense move with one broad shoulder. 'I had—other sources.'

Other sources... 'What other sources?'

'I think you should sit down—'

'I don't want to sit down!' Mia exploded. 'I want to know what business it is of yours what I've been doing! And why you believe you can stand there like a disapproving father, censuring me!'

The moment she finished screeching at him she ruined it all by swaying when her dizzy head protested at the pressure she'd placed on it.

'Sit down!' he barked at her.

'No!' she fired back.

Only to release a groan that turned into a frustrated whimper when her stomach began to heave. Her hand went to cover it, her other hand lifting to hold her dizzy head. She heard Nikos mutter something not very polite about stubborn females, then felt his hands cup her elbows and she was being forcibly guided back down onto the sofa.

Then the doorbell went.

'Stay right there,' Nikos instructed—as if she was in a fit state to go anywhere!—and strode off.

Two minutes later he was back again, walking into the room with a middle-aged man carrying a doctor's bag following in his wake, and Mia was back on her feet again, trying her best to look as if she was bursting with robust health.

'Good afternoon, Miss Balfour,' the doctor greeted briskly. 'How may I help you?'

'I really don't—'

'She is suffering from nausea and extreme spells of dizziness,' Nikos took over with smooth, grim efficiency, then added with all the gracious cool of someone happy to toss a fizzing bomb down at her feet, 'She is also in the early stages of pregnancy.'

CHAPTER NINE

SHE should have fainted again, Mia thought later. It would have been the easiest way to get out of what took place next.

But she didn't faint.

Instead she was forced to endure a second consultation in one day, plus a gentle lecture on consuming the right healthy diet and taking the right kind of rest, exercise and sleep.

Having presented his bomb, Nikos had withdrawn to the window again. Long back presented to the room, jacket shoved back, hands thrust into his trouser pockets. He stood like that, signalling his retreat from proceedings, and Mia could not drag her eyes away from him, the shock he had so neatly delivered on her was so great.

The doctor began a speech about the variances of early pregnancy, though she barely heard a word that he said. And even he was feeling the strain in the atmosphere because it was so suffocatingly tense. He kept on glancing at Nikos, then back to Mia's frozen profile while she stared at Nikos too. It had to be obvious that they were not a joyously expecting couple, overexcited and overanxious about becoming parents.

As he prepared to leave, he expressed one final message. 'The nurturing of a new life is a precious gift that should be cherished. Anything less is an offence to the child itself.'

By then even Nikos was showing cracks in his unyielding demeanour when he turned round and moved to show the doctor out.

And he did not come back.

Mia continued to sit on the sofa, still too stunned to do more than take in the fact that Nikos had somehow managed to grab complete control of the situation before she'd even had a chance to grasp it for herself.

He knew she was pregnant. His *other sources* had been reporting her every move back to him, and by the amount he'd already indicated she had not taken a single step anywhere during the past two weeks without it being carefully tracked.

What was she supposed to make of that?

Suddenly wondering why she was still sitting here like some cowed fool waiting for him to deign to put in an appearance, Mia shot to her feet. Her mouth felt unnaturally dry and her stomach was still not happy but she discovered that she could walk without making the walls and floor move about.

Stepping out of the living room she discovered that the apartment was a lot bigger than she'd expected it to be. A wide central hallway fed right down its middle, with doors leading off from either side of it, most of them thrown open like the doors in his house in Hampshire.

Shivering she turned in the direction of the only closed door—the door out of here. She was going to escape while she had the chance. She needed to use the loo and she desperately needed a drink of something long and cool and thirst quenching. She did *not* need—

'Don't even think about it,' his deep voice arrived with a quiet, seriously threatening undertone to it.

Pulses leaping like mad, Mia pressed her dry lips together and closed her eyes for a second, then opened them again and, folding her arms across her front, turned to look at him.

He was poised half in, half out of a room farther down the hallway. Her guarded blue eyes connected briefly with the narrowed glint reflecting from his, then dropped almost of their own volition down the length of his long lean stance.

He'd removed his suit jacket and his shirt-sleeves had been folded up his forearms. He held what looked like a tea towel in one long-fingered hand. It came to her that she was seeing yet another side to this complicated man, this one being his domesticated side.

Did it distract from the raw sexual male she'd been so fascinated by for so long? No, she admitted helplessly as her tummy flipped for a different reason. Without knowing she was doing it she covered it with a hand.

Lowering his gaze to watch the revealing gesture, Nikos had to fight not to grind his teeth together as anger erupted inside. She was barely managing to stand upright. She looked the colour of paste. She'd lost weight—too much weight going by the way her pale blue cotton dress was hanging on her. And she looked so beautiful and fragile and vulnerable he wanted to leap on her and carry her off to the nearest bed!

Where the hell had he got the idea he could just brush her off like the others?

The clue was in the question, Nikos told himself grimly. She wasn't *like* the others.

She was open, emotional, temperamental and feisty, he listed. Extraordinarily beautiful and soul-destroyingly sexy without knowing that she was. Even now while she stood there trying to maintain an upright position, all he could think about was stripping off that sack of a dress so he could see how much damage two weeks of barely eating had done to her fabulous shape.

And she was pregnant with his child, he tagged on finally. What the hell was sexy about knowing she was pregnant with his child? He had never wanted children. The knowledge of one nestling somewhere inside her should be bringing him out in a cold sweat, but it wasn't.

He had to veil his eyes so she would not see how the powerful stuff pounding around inside him was almost knocking *him* over while he stood here trying to play it cool.

'I'm preparing something to eat as per doctor's orders,' he relayed evenly. 'If you can walk this far without collapsing, come and join me.'

For a second, for a pin-piercing, nerve-tripping second, he thought she was going to launch a second verbal attack on him. She drew in a breath, her chin shot up, her fabulous blue eyes sparked, her gorgeously soft, full, vulnerable mouth parted and the scent for the fight filled his body with a sizzling hot charge that would have only one outlet.

And *that* was the reason why he must have been mad to believe he could brush her off like the others. She fired him up even when he did not want firing up. She fired him up without even knowing she was doing it! She challenged him, fascinated him—annoyed the hell out of him.

'I need to use a bathroom,' she said.

It was like coming down from a drug-induced high. Long fingers gripping the tea towel like it was some kind of lethal weapon, he waved it at a door to her right. 'Second door down,' he indicated.

With that he stepped back into the kitchen and vented some of what was gripping him by tossing the tea towel across the room the moment he knew she couldn't see him do it.

Mia collapsed against the closed bathroom door. She had absolutely no idea what had been going on just now but she felt as if she'd just survived an attack from invisible aliens. Every nerve end she possessed was standing on end and tingling with alarm. He had not moved. He had not said anything particularly contentious. He had not been anything but absolutely casual and cool.

It was her, she told herself. She was so up-tight about these *other sources* she was sensing things about him that just were not there. Trying to pull herself together she turned to lock the door, only to frown when she discovered there wasn't a lock there. Since when did multimillion-pound apartments come with no locks on the bathroom doors?

She was washing her hands when she recalled that the bathroom attached to her bed-room in Hampshire had no lock and neither had the bedroom door. And all of the doors there had been standing wide open, as if the sheer pace of restless energy Nikos always generated meant he needed to move around his homes without the irritating restriction of having to pause to fling open doors.

And that was it, Mia recognised suddenly. All those strange sensations she had been picking up on out there just now had been the sparking trails of his restless energy screaming around the walls, trying to get out, because he had to be feeling so constrained by the ap-palling discovery that she was carrying his child.

He was slicing a knife through a fresh crisp salad sandwich when she presented herself in the doorway. Her unpredictable stomach im-mediately reacted to the delicious smell with a hungry growl.

Glimpsing her hovering there Nikos indi-cated with the knife to one of the high stools set by a marble-topped eating bar. 'Sit down,' he invited.

Reluctant to move any closer to him but too hungry to stay where she was, Mia hitched herself onto the stool.

'Drink,' he said, setting a tall glass of sparkling fresh orange down in front of her. Half the sandwich arrived while she was drinking thirstily from the glass.

'I don't know what you like so I've piled everything in there. Just take out what you don't want to eat.'

In other words, eating nothing was not an option, Mia interpreted. Not that she was thinking of causing a fight about it. She was too hungry.

'I thought you were in Busan,' she said as she set down her glass.

'I flew back overnight.' Lifting up a boiling kettle he poured the water into a stainless-steel cafetière, infusing the room with the rich aroma of freshly ground coffee.

About to pick up the sandwich, her fingers stilled. 'Because you found out I was pregnant,' she prompted.

'Even I cannot see into the future, *agape mou*. You only found out during your visit to your GP this morning.' He sent her a wry glance. 'Though I will admit I suspected it might be the reason for your stomach bug when Fiona relayed her concerns to me about it.'

Mia stared at him. 'Why would you come up with such a suspicion?' She had not thought of it so why should he?

He offered up a shrug. 'I did not use anything.'

Did not use anything? 'Explain this—did not use anything,' she demanded.

To her surprise he let out a short dry laugh. 'Innocent to the last skin cell,' he mocked, turning around to send her a sardonic glance. 'Protection,' he delivered, accentuating each syllable like he was talking to an idiot. 'Contraception,' he added in the same mocking way. 'The protective use of a condom, if you need me to spell it out clearer for you.'

'I do not.' Cheeks heating because she could not believe she had walked herself into that totally embarrassing explanation, she fired at him, 'Why did you *not use anything*? Or do you treat all your one-night stands as cavalierly as you did me?'

'No.' Veiling his eyes, his answer was that short and gruff.

'Then why take such liberties with my body?'

For some reason his mouth moved into a rueful twist. 'Freudian slip,' he said, as if that should make sense to her.

Well, it didn't. '*Grazie*, then, for the care you took with me!'

Nikos said nothing, he just turned back to what he was doing, leaving her anger to bounce off his back. Mia sizzled where she sat for a few seconds longer, unable to absorb that a man like him could take such irresponsible risks! Then she recalled the powerful grip of their mutual passion, and she shifted restlessly on her seat. She had been too busy enjoying herself to give a thought to protection either. She could not pile the entire blame on to him.

'The smell of that coffee is upsetting my stomach,' she announced, and enjoyed watching his disconcerted start before he leapt to snap on an air-extractor fan, then proceeded to flush his preferred beverage down the sink.

Mia bit into her sandwich with relish, having paid him back for his crucifying explanation for *not using anything*. He was always way too arrogantly sure of himself. Discovering he had faults to pick at made her feel much better.

Pouring chilled water into a glass from a bottle he'd removed from the fridge, he came to sit down on the stool next to hers. That brought him too close. Tensing her spine Mia put down the sandwich.

'So who are the other sources you referred to?'

'Security team.' Reaching across to pick up the discarded sandwich, he almost threatened to feed it to her until she took it from his long stubborn fingers. 'You've been under discreet surveillance since the Anton Brunel incident,' he enlightened. 'A precaution both Oscar and I decided was necessary to your—'

'Oscar—?' She swung a horrified blue stare at him. 'You have told Oscar what happened to me?'

'I'm responsible for your safety—'

'*Sì.*' Mia heaved in taut breath. 'I am the *duty* you took on at Oscar's request. You do not have to spell that part out.'

'Why are you angry? We were working in your best interests—'

'By spying on me without telling me you were doing it—and I did not even notice, did I?'

'If you had noticed, then the security team would not have been doing their job properly,' Nikos drawled smoothly.

'Have you been reporting back to Oscar about everything I say and do?' Mia speared at him suddenly. 'Do you have a special tick list for when I perform up to Balfour standards and another one for crosses when I fail to reach the required level of your expectations?'

His brown eyes cooled. 'That wasn't funny, Mia.'

She so agreed with him there! Had he been colluding with Oscar over every step that she took? She hoped not, thinking about the intimacy they shared that had put her in the situation she was in now.

She felt like a curiosity in a zoo, watched and discussed and picked over. 'I wish I had never come to England now,' she breathed, a tremor of hurt tensing her mouth. 'I wish I had never met you.'

'Too late for both wishes,' Nikos said, then let out a short sigh. 'Before you spin me into the manipulative villain here, Oscar called *me*. Santino D'Lassio succeeded in keeping your unplanned dip off the television screens but he was not so successful with the press. Oscar read about it and called me.'

As Sophie had called her, Mia remembered, simmering down a little.

'Together we decided that Brunel could become—a nuisance to you, so I employed a team to watch over you in case the nasty piece of work decided to try something again—and that was *all* Oscar and I discussed.'

'Oh,' she quivered. 'I…th-thank you.'

'I don't need thanking,' Nikos discarded with frowning annoyance. 'It was deemed necessary to your safety so it was done. Of course, I did not expect to find out you were living it up until all hours with Kat Balfour's crazy friends!'

'They are not crazy, and it was only one night!' Mia fired up all over again. 'And what business of yours is it who I see or what I do with my free time? You blew me off. You told me I was a very big mistake!'

'For your own good.'

'It is a very big shame it did not run to contraception too!' Mia threw out with simmering sarcasm.

He straightened his broad shoulders. 'Fair point,' he acknowledged.

Mia wanted to get up and hit him! Instead she heaved in a deep breath, let it out again slowly, then put down the sandwich. 'I can't eat this now,' she sighed.

'My fault again?' He sighed too. 'But at least try to eat it. I promise I won't say another word while you do…doctor's orders,' he reminded her.

Doctor's orders… Because of the baby, he meant. Reluctantly she picked up the sandwich. True to his word, he did not utter another word while she ate. When she'd finished he pushed her glass towards her in a silent command for her to finish that too.

'Tulio has nothing on you,' she sniped, snatching up the glass.

To her surprise he husked out a soft laugh. 'I'm beginning to like Tulio,' he confided. 'He sounds like my kind of guy. I'll look forward to meeting him when we go to visit your aunt…'

Mia looked at him, deeply suspicious as to where he was leading her with that cool statement. The moment she made contact with his rich dark eyes and saw a golden light burning there, it made her shift tensely on the stool.

What was he up to—what was he thinking? Why was she reading the glint as the burn of promised complete and total possession in those eyes—so much so that she began to feel threatened?

Mia moistened her lips and felt them tingle when he lowered his eyes to watch the careful little gesture.

'No.' She shook her head. 'You are not going anywhere near Tia Giulia.'

He took his time bringing his eyes back up to hers. 'Why not?' he asked softly.

A sizzling fizz of heat began to fire deep down in her body. That there was something else going on here as well as the conversation they were involved in, made her flicker a wary scan of his face. He was leading her somewhere and she did not want to look at where that might be.

How did a man so famous for his cool self-control manage to transmit so much sexual tension without seeming to try—?

'I would be too ashamed to present you to her,' she said.

And hit a raw nerve. Mia watched that warm possessive golden light turn off like a switch. He leant back on the stool. It was like watching a dangerous animal take a serious blow it had not been prepared for, and she suddenly felt really bad for saying what she did.

'*Tia* is going to be ashamed of me too,' she added in what was a huskily spoken soother to the wounded beast. 'And—and anyway, there is no reason why the two of you should m-meet.'

'No,' she thought she heard him utter from the deep dark recesses of his taut throat.

The atmosphere in the kitchen had suddenly gone somewhere Mia knew she did not want to follow. In fact, she decided without rhyme or reason as to why it hit her at this particular moment, she just knew she did not want to be here with him any longer.

Her slender fingers gripping the glass, she downed the rest of her orange, then put the glass down and slid off the stool. Nikos still was not moving and she was feeling distinctly threatened as she took a wary step towards the kitchen door.

'Going somewhere?' his deep voice questioned.

'T-to my own apartment...' She took another step.

'We still have a lot to talk about,' Nikos drawled.

Not if she could avoid it. 'I'm—too tired to talk to you any more today,' she said coolly. 'We—we can talk again tomorrow.'

'Too late then. We have plans to make before tomorrow.'

Mia nipped in a taut breath, then spun around. He'd recovered quickly enough from his wounds, was the first observation that leapt out at her, though he did still look strained around his mouth.

'I don't know what is the matter with you,' she said, adding a flick of a hand to convey her helpless bewilderment. 'What is the planning you speak about? We don't have to plan anything! And you should be drowning your sorrows somewhere in a bottle of whisky instead of playing this silly game with me!'

'No game,' he denied.

'Then where exactly do you think you are going with this?' she burst out, asking the question she had been trying to run away from.

'I know exactly where I'm going with it, *cara*,' Nikos responded grimly. 'Even with the crushing knock-back,' he added with a twist of his taut mouth, 'I am simply waiting for you to catch up with me.'

He was still seated on the stool with his long legs stretched out in front of him, looking for the world now like he was set to stay there like that for the rest of the day. But it was all just a big deception. Mia could still see that telling gleam in his eyes, a *burn* which reminded her of—

She took a step backwards. 'S-stop looking at me like that—'

He arched one of his flat black eyebrows. 'Like what?'

'Like you…' Running out of words she dragged in a tense breath of air and looked away.

'Like I'm considering—other options to help you to catch up with me?'

He was thinking *sex*, Mia saw, though she did not want to. In the space of a few short minutes he'd gone from domestic animal to wounded animal, and now he was displaying the *sexual* animal.

'This is an—improper conversation to be having in—in the middle of a crisis,' Mia said primly.

'I'm having improper urges,' he came back quick as a flash.

Shocked by it, Mia gasped, her eyes widening and her pulse accelerating as he came to his feet.

'Don't you dare to come near me!' She took another jerky step backwards and her spine made painful contact with the corner of the door frame. 'Ouch,' she jerked out.

'Now look what you've done,' Nikos murmured, walking forward to reach out to draw her towards him while Mia made a weak flailing attempt to ward him off. 'You're so fevered and flustered you hurt yourself. Much safer here,' he said, folding her in against his warm hard frame.

A single night of passion with him had not prepared her for the shockingly patent physical evidence of his aroused state pressing against her. Surprised by the inner surge of heat which poured from her towards that contact, she swayed her hips away from him in sheer self-defence.

He used the flat of his hand to bring her back to him again, and smiled at her stifled gasp. 'At last you've caught me up.'

'N-no,' she denied it.

He bent his dark head and touched the tip of his tongue to the corner of her trembling mouth. It was Mia who turned that teasing touch into a full-on kiss. It was she who pressed the already stinging tips of her breasts into his chest and floated her arms up around his neck.

His arms banded her to him. He prized her mouth open and ruthlessly deepened the kiss. If she had a single ounce of pride she would be fighting him like crazy, but hectic little whimpers of pleasure were rolling from her instead.

'I am not going to bed with you!' she shrilled up at him during a moment of separation when he reached up to drag her hair free of its clip.

'The floor will do for me, *amore mia*,' he countered huskily, helping her hair to tumble over his fingers. 'The wall, the sofa, the kitchen table, even the door behind you.'

'And stop talking to me in Italian,' she shook out, shocked by his cool declaration and terribly excited by it at the same time.

'You understand Italian better when you're out of your head with pleasure,' he confided, flaming her a hot mocking look. 'I spent several very passionate hours loving you in Italian and you did not notice my testing efforts, did you? Shame on you, Mia. This time I will make love to you in Greek and you will wish by the time I have finished that you had bothered to learn my language!'

'You're mad. W-we can't do this—'

'Why not?'

'I'm s-sick—'

'With pining for me,' he agreed. 'Well, you're pining is over, *agapita*.' Something soft hit the backs of her knees and she collapsed onto a bed. She did not know how they'd even got here! Her arms jerked up around his shoulders on a startled shriek. 'That's right,' he encouraged. 'Cling to me, you are going to need me to keep you this close to stop from drowning.'

Her eyes fluttered open. 'Why are you *doing* this?'

Lifting his dark head, Nikos looked down at her, eyes as black as midnight in his taut face. 'Because you've got me, *cara*, even if you're ashamed of me. Now I'm going to love you senseless before I take you somewhere and marry you.'

Marriage—did he say *marriage*—? 'I'm not marrying you!' she cried out shockingly. 'No way!'

He took her lips with a hot driving hunger that devoured her ability to protest any more. Mia tried to hang on to her sanity but he robbed her of it as he explored her mouth with the sensuous force of a ruthless raider. She felt as if she was being consumed by his desire. She should be fighting him. She knew she should be fighting him, but the only urge flowing through her was the urge to rake her fingers through his hair and to apply pressure to his head to stop him from breaking the hot deep hungry kiss.

She didn't even know where it had all come from. One minute they were fighting, the next minute eating, the next they were here on his bed making love with the kind of fever that should be shocking her stupid, but instead she was revelling in it. For days now she had walked around like a car accident, stunned by the way he'd enthralled her with his passion, then dumped her without a single qualm. Now here she lay being enthralled again as if all the hurt and rejection meant nothing at all!

He skimmed a restless hand down her body and located a silken slender thigh exposed because her dress had ridden up to her waist. The feather-light brush of his caress set her squirming against him and he muttered something hard and impatient, used his other hand to lift her up towards him, then without breaking the passionate seal of their lips, he ran down the zip of her dress. Cool air hit her skin and she shivered. In the next second she was breaking her mouth free on a cry of protest as he wrenched the pale blue cotton downwards, forcing her to let go of him so he could free it from her slender arms as it was trailed away.

Her lacy white bra drew the heat of his attention, and with breathtaking economy it sprang free and it too was being trailed away, revealing the firm fullness of her breasts with their twin tight peaks posing like shameless provocateurs.

'Oh,' Mia groaned and closed her eyes as he lowered his dark head and took one straining tip into his mouth, her fingers clawing at his shoulders when she just went wild.

As if her clutching fingers reminded him he was still wearing his clothes, he muttered something and reared back, wrenching impatiently at his shirt. Buttons flew in all directions. Opening her eyes she was shocked to see the amount of angry hot furious tension clenched in the muscles in his face.

'Why are you so angry?' she whispered.

'I messed up with you,' he answered harshly. 'I don't mess up.'

Rolling off the bed he stood so he could rid himself of the rest of his clothes.

'Marriage was not on my agenda, nor were children,' he muttered, raking his trousers off his body to display the astonishing beauty of his long tanned physique presented in its fully aroused state.

Mia touched the trembling tip of her tongue to her upper lip in sheer siren hunger. 'I have not placed marriage on your agenda, Nikos.'

'If I'm stuck with it, then you're stuck with it. *Theos*,' he groaned, coming back down to her. 'I've been aching to do this again.'

It was like being handed a gift she had not been expecting, so Mia rewarded him with a passionate kiss. He'd wanted her. He'd flown around the world and ached for her. She was so exhilarated by that confession she forgot to continue the other subject.

The marriage subject.

Instead she let him sink her down into a deep dark well shored up with pure sensation. His touch was sheer tormenting pleasure. Clever and light, so sensually expert at driving her towards that screaming-pitch peak.

She raked his back with her fingernails. He set her sobbing with his mouth on her breasts. He made her touch him. He fed her hand down the length of his long body in a stirring trail that followed the virile line of dark curls to the velvet hard shock of his erection. He taught her how to send shudders of pleasure raking through him. When he made that first silken thrust inside her she felt the leash he had placed on himself shake his entire frame. He was hot, his skin moist with sweat, his lips trembling against hers and she clung to him, clung like she was in danger of drowning if she ever let go.

Now what? Mia wondered as she lay curled on her side, watching him move about the room. Another ruthless slap down in case she got romantic ideas about his feelings? Another grim demand for marriage she neither wanted nor was about to accept?

He had already showered but had not yet bothered to dress. A small towel rested low on his waist, hiding his tight narrow buttocks and clashing wonderfully with his deep bronzed skin.

'When you've rested, you need to go and

pack a bag,' he said, lifting clean underwear out of a drawer.

'Why,' she asked warily. 'Where am I going?'

'Athens,' he answered. 'It's time you saw how we run things from my main base.'

And that was it? No—go and buy a wedding dress? No return to the marriage subject at all? Curving a hand beneath her cheek, Mia said nothing, her eyelashes resting low across her eyes as she watched him move to a bank of wardrobes.

'And it's time you met the guy whose job you filched,' he continued evenly, pulling a striped blue-and-white shirt on over his fabulous torso and making Mia pull a disappointed face. 'Fortunately for Petros, he's enjoyed staying behind in Athens, taking my place while I've been elsewhere.'

'So he is not likely to want to beat me up.'

Fastening the top button on the shirt, he turned a glance on her. *Belissimo*, Mia thought. Sexy, she thought. Those lazy satiated love-darkened eyes should be censored—or kept right here in the bedroom with me.

'You look like a long sleek golden cat lying there.' He smiled at her.

Her heart tippled over, then gave a soft squeeze because he was not being cold with her, and the way he had not been looking at her while he talked had made her expect his cool detachment.

'My hair is black,' she pointed out.

'I wasn't referring to your hair, *agape mou*.'

Mia did not know she could blush all the way from her toes, but that was what she did. Nikos saw it and laughed as he strode across the room to the bed. He leant over her, smelling clean of soap and Nikos, and his slow intimate kiss tasted of mint.

'No,' he husked when she reached for him as he went to straighten again. 'We haven't got time for what you want us to do, little cat.' Bending down he picked up her dress and dropped it on her. 'You have an hour to get ready before we have to leave.'

Ignoring her disappointed pout he strode back to the wardrobes to select the pants to a navy suit. As he drew them up his legs and Mia sat up with all the reluctance of someone who did not want to go anywhere, he murmured, 'And you will need to give me your birth certificate. Do you have it with you here?'

'Yes, with my passport, but—' she frowned '—I don't understand why you need it.'

'Marriage licence,' he responded as cool as anything. 'We will be married in Athens next week. Petros is already seeing to the arrangements.'

CHAPTER TEN

'DON'T sulk,' her tormentor chided coolly.

Mia unclenched her tightly clenched teeth. 'I have told you before, I do not sulk,' she denied stiffly.

'Then look at me.'

Twisting her face around, Mia did as he commanded, only to feel the unwanted pull of his sexual magnetism descend on her like a stifling hot weight. He was just so—*bello*, she thought helplessly, his luxurious black hair, his liquid dark eyes, his firm sensually moulded mouth. The barely leashed power of his fiercely masculine physique clothed in a sense-stirringly casual iron-grey silk lounge suit and gorgeously body-moulding black T-shirt.

How was she supposed to continue to fight with him when even his long lounging posture in the plush leather limo seat next to her wound up her sexual cravings for him to the extent she hardly dare breathe in case she gave herself away.

'Well,' she said. 'I am looking. Say what it is you want to say so I can look away again.'

His sensual mouth moved to a slow mocking tilt. 'Why, when you love looking at me?'

The pounding throb of her stubborn refusal to take up that goading remark sparked from her blue eyes like electricity. She'd maintained the same stance since they left London. Now they were driving across Athens on their way to dinner at some fancy restaurant when she would much rather have locked herself away in her bedroom.

Only Nikos's Athens apartment had no locks on the bedroom doors, did it? Mia thought as she seethed.

They'd maintained an armed truce while they'd dressed to go out again—she shut away in her allotted bedroom, Nikos shut away in his. And that arrangement in itself made a complete laughing mockery of what it was they were warring about.

The marriage thing, being the bone of contention. He refused to take no for an answer and she refused to say yes.

'Will you just explain to me why you are being so stubborn about this,' he demanded heavily.

Mia had at least a dozen reasons why, but the only one she was prepared to give him right now needed just two words. 'Lois Mansell,' she said, and waited for him to squirm.

But he did not squirm. He did not do anything other than to sustain steady eye contact with her like a smooth rat caught in a trap who arrogantly did not believe he had anything to squirm about!

'Lois has nothing to do with us,' he dismissed that line of argument.

'The newspapers told it differently.'

'You know all about newspapers, *cara*. They lie—or at the very least they tamper with the truth.'

'You left that nightclub with her clinging to you like a limpet.' Mia was unimpressed by his line of defence.

'I delivered her home. I did not sleep with her.'

'The way I see it, Nikos, you don't *sleep* with any of your women.'

As a stab at their current sleeping arrangements Mia knew she'd hit her mark when his dark eyes shuttered and his mouth went tight.

'No response?' she sniped at him. 'No smart comeback aimed to put me in my place?'

'No,' he murmured, looking away from her altogether.

'Well, there you are, then.' *She* looked away too. 'You and I do not have the same view as to what marriage is supposed to be about.'

'You're pregnant with my child,' he clipped out. 'Such an event does not require mutual insight, it requires damage control.'

'Damage control—?' So hurt by that comment, she could not hold in her choked gasp. 'And you wonder why I won't say yes to you when you can come out with a cold statement like that?'

'I'm trying to be practical—'

'As you have been with our sleeping arrangements?' She could not resist saying it, then yanked in a tight breath. 'You get me pregnant. You expect me to marry you. But you don't want to sleep in the same bed as me,' she shook out. 'I suppose you will also expect to continue to live your life as you have always done while I sit at home alone getting fat!'

'So what do you want?' he angled back at her.

A man who wants to marry me because he cannot live without me! Mia screamed inside her head. 'Not a man who thinks of marriage as damage control,' she muttered. 'I would rather return to Italy and bring my child up alone than throw my life away on a man like that.'

'*Our* child,' he gritted out. 'And you are going nowhere with or without the marriage. I will bring up my own child, Mia,' he stated very grimly. 'I will not let your silly stubborn truculence push me out of the frame over some—crazy issues you have about the quality of my commitment.'

The problem was there was no quality about it! Hurt tears clogged her throat. 'Can we go back?' she husked. 'I don't think I can eat anything.'

His growling sigh was driven. 'You are such damn high maintenance—!' he raked out.

Mia widened her blue eyes in simmering astonishment. 'I don't believe that you dared to say that!' she choked. 'I have cost you nothing! Not even the price of accommodation since the flat I used in London was yours anyway and was already standing vacant!'

'I did not mean—'

'Shut up!' she heaved out. 'You know what you are, Nikos?' she hit back at him shakily. 'You are an arrogant, selfish—cheapskate!' Almost tumbling over the word because she was not certain she had said it correctly, she knew she'd hit the word exactly right when he tensed like a board and pushed up his aggressive chin.

'So I f-fancied you—big deal,' she railed on an angry high now. 'So you condescended to take what I was putting on offer— Great, thank you, *grazie tanto*, *amore mia*—not! For what did it cost you? A reasonably priced dinner and a few hours of listening to me bore you to death, followed by a posh party and a swift bit of pleasure in your bed before you turned on me like an ice man and threw me out! If that makes me high maintenance, then may God forgive you for what you usually shower on to your women! No wonder they say beware of Greeks bearing gifts!'

'Have you finished?' the ice man delivered from between his clenched white teeth. 'If so, then may I finish what I was about to say *before* you blew my head off? Yes? *Sì? Ne?*' His sarcasm ripped like a razor through Mia's trembling flesh. 'I was about to add *emotionally*,' he incised with deliberate precision. 'High maintenance *emotionally*,' he repeated. 'And a bloody irritating pain in the neck!'

'Don't forget juvenile!' Mia tagged on for herself.

The car came to a standstill. Without uttering another word Nikos opened his door and threw himself out. Mia continued to sit, simmering in silence, while she waited for him to come around and open her door. She could have got out under her own steam but she did not want to. If she had been given a choice—and he had allowed her very few choices over the past twelve hours— she would be staying right where she was!

'Leave the temper in the car,' he rasped as she arrived in front of him.

Refusing to give such a command mind space, Mia tossed her hair back from her face with an icy defiance that made Nikos grit his teeth.

Women were an absolute blast, he thought angrily as they walked together across the pavement towards one of the most exclusive eating establishments in town. They did not know when to behave themselves—or when a man had taken enough of their unbelievably volatile and inconsistent nonsense! She had not been so argumentative when he'd brought her down to straddle him during the flight over here and kissed her snappy mouth.

And, *Theos*, this was not the time to be recalling what they'd done next, when she was already firing him up again, because she looked nothing short of dazzling in full angry flow! Her eyes were alight, her mouth pumped and pouting because he'd cornered her just before they left his apartment and tried to kiss her out of her stubbornness. The kiss had been yet another ground-shaking experience—without the satisfying follow-up because her stubborn shell remained fixed in place.

But her sensational mouth still wore his kiss on it in defiance—and he wanted to kiss it again, right now!

'Take care,' he husked, taking hold of her arm as she went to negotiate the shallow step in front of the restaurant entrance.

She was wearing the usual lethal high heels and he made a silent promise to himself that he was going to chuck them all out the first opportunity he got! She was pregnant, for God's sake. Carrying his baby. One accidental stumble off those ridiculous heels and it could all be over—

Something shockingly like panic struck down through his body, pulling him to a shuddering halt. Mia glanced up at him in frowning surprise and his heart made a weird kind of dive down to his toes.

'What?' she asked, glaring at him as if she was expecting yet another row to erupt.

'Nothing,' he said, pulling himself together. 'I just remembered something I should have done before we left,' he lied, feeling strangely light-headed as he reached around her to open the restaurant door.

She walked ahead of him into the foyer with a curvaceous glide of purple satin, short and fitted and fashionably edgy, her fabulous hair a silken stream of black waves that brushed her tense narrow back.

Purple for poison or purple for passion, he mused grimly. Tonight she was both.

The owner of the restaurant came hurrying up to greet him. He had to pull on his social face when he did not want to, smiling pleasantly while Mia stood beside him, thankfully donning her social smile too. So he'd taught her something, Nikos thought with bleak satire.

They were about to move on through to the restaurant proper when the door flew open and a group of newcomers came in. It was instinct that made him turn to send them a fleeting glance.

Nikos froze as an icy shaft of instant recognition locked up his muscles. No, he thought, this cannot be happening. He tried to deflect Mia's attention when she turned to see where he was looking, but he was too late and she froze too.

'We will leave,' he husked, already reaching out to draw her protectively towards him.

'No.' Feeling as if the ground beneath her feet was trembling, Mia let him hold her for a moment.

But it wasn't the ground, it was she who was trembling, shivery chills of shock tingling up and down her spine.

Gabriella.

Gabriella was right here in this place, in this city, standing a short metre away from her. Her mother, looking so agonizingly familiar to her because she saw that face in the mirror each time she looked at herself.

Her heart began to thump out of kilter. She felt Nikos trying his best to block her view with the long length of his body and his wide shoulders. And she knew he was doing it because she must have turned the colour of milk.

'I'm going to speak to her,' she whispered.

The decision came without her even knowing she wanted to do such a thing.

'No—Mia, don't,' Nikos advised gruffly. 'You—'

But she was already stepping round him on legs that did not feel like they belonged to her any more. Mario Mattea glanced at her and he knew—that quickly he knew who it was he was looking at.

Tall and lean, strikingly attractive for a man in his sixtieth year, he touched his wife's arm to gain her attention. 'Gabriella,' he murmured in a low warning voice.

Gabriella Mattea turned her luxurious dark head and looked into the pale face of the daughter she had not set eyes on in ten long years.

Silence poured into the gap between them. Mia felt her heart take on a thick pounding beat in her ears. Somewhere in the hazy distance she was aware of Nikos's tension and of Mario's. There were other people around them but they were invisible; she only saw her mother's face.

Feeling as vulnerable as the small child she had been when she last stood this close to her mother, she whispered tremulously, '*Ciao, M-Mama.*'

Eyes like black glass looked her over. Mia watched the beautiful face in front of her freeze.

'For goodness' sake, will someone get this person away from me?' Gabriella drawled out in cold Italian. 'Is it impossible to eat out without being set upon by strangers these days?'

A stunning silence fell around the foyer. In the middle of it Mia slowly died. Then Nikos's arm was a fierce brace across her shoulders. And Mario was bursting into speech.

'Nikos,' he greeted tensely. 'I did not expect to see you—'

'Excuse us,' Nikos cut in coldly and walked them to the door.

The restaurant owner leapt to open it for them, murmuring apologies in a shocked anxious voice. They made it onto the pavement. So coldly furious he could hit something, Nikos speared a glance up the street, looking for where his driver had parked.

Turning his shaking frozen package towards him he wrapped her in one supporting arm, pressing her close against his body, while he located his mobile phone. Keeping his anger in check cost him control of his voice as he ordered his driver to come and get them.

'Nikos, please.' Mario appeared on the pavement beside them. 'Let me explain to you why that unfortunate scene happened,' he begged urgently. 'My wife—'

'An explanation is not required,' Nikos sliced

through the other man, his arm banding Mia all the tighter to him. 'It happened because you gave Gabriella a choice and she chose you, your wealth and your lifestyle over her own child.' As Nikos spoke, Mia quivered in fresh hurt as he outlined the stark cold truth of it. 'It happened,' he continued, 'because you and your wife are soulless, with a soulless marriage, which in my view makes you well suited. Mia might not appreciate this right now but she has been better off without knowing either of you.'

'Because she has Balfour to turn to now?' Mario's sudden harsh derision cut into Mia like a knife.

'No,' Nikos countered. 'Because she has me.'

The car swept to a stop beside them, and Nikos reached out to open the rear door. There was a new atmosphere rocking the silence which hung in the warm evening, but Mia was too upset to work out why it was there. She let Nikos guide her into the limousine, and tried very hard to get a grip on herself. In truth she should not be feeling this bad, she told herself. After all, she was the one at fault for thinking she could approach a woman who had never shown the slightest hint that she cared about her.

The two men were still standing on the pavement. From the low grind of their voices Mia could tell their conversation was not nice. A quick glance showed her that Nikos's whole body was rigid with aggression and icy as hell. Mario seemed to be pressing some urgent point and looked very pale, though she did not know the wealthy formula-one mogul to know he did not always look that shade.

She looked away again, down at her trembling fingers where they lay locked together on her lap. Nikos was right—who needed a mother like that? she told herself dimly, and felt tears press hard at the back of her throat.

Nikos climbed into the car and tapped on the partition glass to tell their driver to go. As he sank back into the seat he did not glance at Mia. He couldn't right now. He was too busy grappling with something he'd said to Mario in his initial volley of contempt that was still knocking him almost senseless.

Soulless marriage...

Isn't that what he had been offering Mia? A soulless marriage with great sex and separate bedrooms afterwards?

Nikos shuddered in disgust. She possessed more integrity than her lousy mother by refusing what he was fast accepting had been a filthy insult of an offer. If Gabriella had held out against Mario Mattea, would she have won her man and kept her child—?

And even the thought was insultingly arrogant. For what would Mia be winning by getting him? Nothing more than he had been prepared to give her, which turned out to be nothing in the cold light of his new insight.

He should be getting down on his knees and thanking her for loving this cold and soulless bastard—

Love… Nikos backtracked, experiencing a fresh numbing clench of shock. She loved him. How long had he known that without allowing himself to acknowledge it? Desire, obsession, infatuation—he'd named it any other word he could grab. But she did—love him. And he did not deserve such an honour.

'You know him,' the silent figure beside him broke into the shattering train of his thoughts.

'Sorry?' he turned a questioning look on her and took the full weight of her importance to him like a blow to his gut.

'You know Mario Mattea,' she repeated, her blue eyes dull and dark in her pale face. 'Why have you never said?'

Shot down but still functioning, Nikos recognised ruefully as her question pushed him out of one stark blinding revelation straight into the horror of another one. Did he tell her the truth or did he try to pass it off with a flippant comment. *Lie*, in other words.

He veiled his eyes and went for the half-truth. 'I know a lot of business people,' he said with a shrug.

'Have you met my—Gabriella before?'

'No.' And that was honest, Nikos mocked grimly. If he had met Gabriella Mattea before he would have recognised the cold bitch in her and perhaps been able to save Mia from what just took place. As it was, Nikos knew, right down to his seething twisting gut, he was in trouble here.

'He's here in Athens to set up a series of meetings with high-end financiers.' He chickened out of telling the full truth. 'The credit crunch has bitten hard into the car industry. Mario is desperate for someone to finance his business and his formula-one team before both sink without a trace.'

'You mean he's here for a series of meetings with you, don't you?'

Nikos let his tense mouth stretch into a brief rueful smile. 'I'm—one of his best bets to cough up the money.'

'Are you going to?'

He sent her a glinting look. 'What do you think?'

'Because of me?'

'Yes, because of you.' And that was the full damn truth.

'But you can't do that!' Surprising him by

turning an aghast stare on him, she said, 'They will know you turned away from them because of what happened tonight and they will blame me for it!'

His grim face toughened. 'They should have considered that angle when they humiliated my future wife.'

'I am not going to be your wife!'

'What are you planning to be, then,' he struck back, 'the next Balfour scandal?'

CHAPTER ELEVEN

WRONG thing to say. Nikos knew it the moment the smart shot left his mouth.

'I am *not* a Balfour,' Mia denied, hating him for saying that—hating everyone. 'For why would I want to be a Bianchi or a Balfour?'

'Then don't be,' he persisted. 'Be a Theakis instead.'

'So that you can treat me like an unwelcome interloper into your life too?'

'You would not be an unwelcome interloper.'

Mia released a soft bitter laugh. 'I am a figure of pity to you right now. Tomorrow I will be a chain tied around your neck. Do you think I don't know the way that it goes? Gabriella handed me over to my aunt, then walked away from me. She visited once a year for the first ten years of my life. She *stopped* visiting me when I asked her if she only came to give *Tia* money for my keep. You wish to hear her answer?'

'No,' Nikos muttered.

'She admitted to my face it was so, then left. *Tia*'s money came by post from then on.'

A soft curse raked Nikos's throat. 'She is a selfish bitch with—'

'*Sì,*' Mia cut in on him quickly because she did not need him to tell her what her own mother was. 'Oscar was more subtle. He allowed me to stay so long as I hid in the kitchen and played his housekeeper.'

'He was protecting Lillian—'

'You think I don't know and appreciate that?' she choked out. 'Do you think I resented him protecting his poor wife's feelings over mine? Do you think I did not understand when his other daughters must resent and blame me for the scandals which erupted later—or that I do not blame myself for those same events? But did *he* appreciate how I was feeling?' she delivered with a hurt that until now she had kept buried deep inside. 'Did my feelings stop him from sending me away again as quickly as he could?'

'Oscar wanted you to learn to—'

'He wanted me to act like a *Balfour* or stay away,' she wrenched out. 'Well, I have no wish any longer to be a Balfour.' And she meant it— she really meant it! 'They are not my kind of people. *You* are not my kind of people.' It was a life-changing moment to realise that and it grew like a balloon inside. 'Oscar said he wanted me to learn integrity…' And suddenly she understood what integrity meant to *her*. It meant being true to *herself*. To the person *she* wanted to be not the one everyone else wanted to mould her into! 'Well, I don't want his integrity if it means dressing up in fine clothes and wearing false smiles. I don't want to be married to you because I have conceived your baby and you are worried about what Oscar might think. That is for your integrity to deal with, Nikos. Mine is telling me it is time to walk away and just be *myself*.'

'I do not give a damn what Oscar thinks!' Nikos protested.

'Liar,' she shook out. 'You have already said it with your damage-control quip.'

It was like being hit from behind. Nikos had not expected it. He had no ready defence.

The car drew up outside his apartment, and Mia threw his sternly handsome face a single glance, then unlocked her seat belt and scrambled out of the car, leaving Nikos sitting there, knowing he was in danger of missing probably the only opportunity he was going to get to put right something he should never have said in the first place.

Throwing open his door he climbed out of the car and followed her into the building. If she wanted him to feel like the worst man alive, then she was succeeding, he accepted as he stood beside her trembling figure while they rode the lift to the top floor.

No oval lobby here, just direct access to his apartment proper.

'Mia...' he started to say huskily.

She strode off towards the bedrooms with her taut slender spine telling him she did not want to listen to anything else he had to say.

He watched her go, watched his chance to put this right walk away from him on those foolish high heels, winced when her bedroom door slammed shut in her wake.

'Damn,' he cursed, then added a few more rich words, and on a ferocious act of burning frustration aimed directly at himself and his own insecurities, he swung around and flung a clenched fist at the nearest wall.

Kicking off her shoes, Mia sent them skidding across the bedroom floor, then spun to glare at the bed for a tear-stinging second before she threw herself face down on it. She hated him—again, she told herself fiercely, pressing her face into the pillow and trembling with anger and a million different layers of hurt.

He was hard and cold and he did not deserve *any* of this aching love she was suffering on his behalf! He did not deserve her at all!

Damage control... What kind of man was he that he could describe a marriage proposal as—

Her door suddenly burst open. 'All right, so the damage-control quip was a lousy, cruel, rotten cover-up!' Nikos launched at her. 'You are driving me crazy. You make me say things I don't mean to say! I think I might be madly in love with you—does that make a difference?'

Mia froze, and then twisted over to look at him. He was standing just inside the door, looking like a man who'd been subjected to torture to make him say that. Every bone, every muscle, every beautifully toned golden skin cell, flexed to its limits, and his eyes were firing fury at her as if she had been the one to inflict the torture!

Had it been that painful for him to say it?

'Explain this *might be*,' she demanded. 'You think it impresses me?'

'No,' he muttered, and did a strange thing then—he dropped the tension out of his shoulders and lifted a fist up to his mouth, wincing as if he was in pain. 'Having never experienced any kind of love before, I can only offer a *might be*,' he said.

Dropping the hand out of its fist he flexed the long fingers. 'You like to believe you are the only one to get a lousy deal in the parental stakes, *agape mou*,' he imparted heavily, 'but you don't have a clue how bad it can get. My mother was a prostitute and my father was her pimp. Try comparing that coupling with your own less-than-perfect parents.'

'But I thought you were—'

'Born with a silver spoon in my mouth?' he offered, skimming her a skin-peeling cynical glance. 'Living in a one-bedroom cockroach-infested apartment deep in the heart of an Athens slum is not silver-spoon stuff, I promise you. It's the same as living in hell. I need a drink,' he said suddenly and turned back to the door.

'Don't you dare walk out of here after saying all of that!' Mia shrieked. 'I want to know what it is you're talking about!'

His wide shoulders clenched. Nikos bit out a curse, then spun to walk over to the window and stood there, glaring out at the view.

'Down there,' he husked, bringing Mia sliding off the bed to go and stand beside him, 'beyond the bright lights where everything turns murky and dark.'

Mia looked without seeing because seeing was not as important to her as what he was saying to her. She moved closer to him and was surprised when he let her, even shifting a tense arm to draw her in.

'For the first six years of my life I believed it was normal to sleep in a bedroom cupboard,' he provided gruffly. 'They, my so-called parents, locked me in there so I would not embarrass my mother's—clients when she brought them back to—ply her services. If I made a sound I was beaten.'

'Oh, Nikos, no,' Mia whispered in dismay.

'They were heroin addicts,' he delivered flatly. 'Sometimes they would be so out of their heads they would forget about me for days. I still have nightmares about that filthy cupboard,' he breathed grittily, then vented a short hard laugh. 'Try sleeping a whole night in the same bed with me, *cara*, and you will know what it is I'm talking about. I cannot stand to be in small enclosed places, and locks and bolts give me the creeps. And don't weep,' he rasped when a sob of understanding broke free from her. 'I will not be responsible if you start weeping. I have told no one this. So just stand here and listen. When I was nine, a—client discovered me. He decided it would be good to have a bit of fun at my expense…'

He went so silent then that Mia worried what it was he was remembering that he could not bring himself to reveal. After a minute of it she could not stand still any longer and turned herself fully into his front, then hugged him tightly with her arms locked around his taut body.

He ripped out a sigh and wrapped his arms around her too.

'I ran away,' he went on. 'The police found me and I was delivered into the hands of the social services. I was never so glad about anything,' he admitted. 'For the first time in my life I had a real bed to sleep in and three meals a day, and most importantly, I felt safe. I was a model inmate because I was so scared they would send me back to my parents. I excelled at school and was willing to take on any chore if it earned me a smile of approval. I would have begged and crawled to remain where I was.'

'Nikos—'

'No, don't say anything,' he cut across her. 'When I was thirteen I was accused of stealing provisions from the kitchens. It wasn't me, I was stitched up, but since I couldn't prove that, I was—punished. I vowed it would be the last time that anyone would lay a strap to my back and I ran away again. I spent the next six months living on the streets, sleeping in alleyways and surviving on meagre handouts. But I missed school. I had a desperate need to learn so I gave myself up to the authorities. From then on I was labelled a problem child and was sent to a home full of problem children...'

He paused once again to take a minute to

smooth out the roughened tone of his voice. And Mia took her chance, and brushed a soft trembling kiss to one of his taut cheeks.

'I endured the life there,' he continued, easing her closer to him. 'I cannot be charitable and call it anything more than an endurance, but I had to stay if I wanted to attend school... The worst part was surrendering to my vow and allowing someone else to beat me,' he roughed out. 'On my sixteenth birthday I walked out of there and never went back.'

'I'm sorry,' she whispered.

'I am not after your sympathy,' he lanced out. 'I am merely trying to explain to you why I cannot tell if I love you or not.' Since Mia was sure that nothing less than the desperation of love would have dragged any of this out of him, she just lifted her face from his chest and smiled up at him. 'Well, I know I love you. So we can work on that.'

Allowing himself to look down at her, Nikos quirked a flat black eyebrow. 'Just like that?'

'*Sì.*' She nodded. 'What happened to your parents?' she then prompted softly.

He cleared his throat. 'They died when I was fourteen, from a lethal batch of heroin.'

'And—and Oscar, how did you come to meet him?'

This time he husked out a small laugh. 'I was

a real hustler by then. Good-looking, sharp-witted and too damn cocksure of myself for my own good. Waiting on tables of the rich was a good place to learn about business scams. I had become pretty successful at scamming others by the time Oscar wandered into my life. I tried a hustle on him,' he admitted. 'Oscar listened to my pitch, fed my ego with smooth questions I was able to answer without so much as a blink. He agreed to the deal, handed me a cheque for an astonishing amount of money, then he proceeded to hustle me with an offer of a stake in some irresistible venture of his own *if* I could come up with the required cash, which was, of course, double what he had given me. I handed him back his cheque plus every penny I had in the world and the scammer had been beautifully scammed by an expert at it.'

Mia laughed. 'You mean there was no irresistible venture?'

'No.' Nikos smiled to himself, recalling what Oscar must have seen when he'd stared thoughtfully across the desk at the twenty-year-old hustler he had been back then. 'Oscar fleeced me cold with a relaxed smoothness that can still make me squirm to recall it,' he confessed.

Yet, for all of it, Oscar Balfour had seen something in him that he'd liked.

'Instead of slinging me out, humiliated and penniless, he offered to show me how to play the hustle from the right side of the law,' he went on softly. 'He was my saviour from a life of crime and probably regular imprisonment. Everything I am today I owe to him. He's— special. Never underestimate him, *agape mou*, for Oscar never puts any plan into action unless he has a very sure idea what the outcome will be.'

'You're talking about you and me now, aren't you?' Mia frowned up at him.

'Right down to the Brunel incident,' he drawled sardonically.

Mia widened her eyes. 'No,' she denied.

'Brunel went overboard with his brief when he tipped you into that pool, and Oscar was angry. But it was Santino D'Lassio's security people who tracked Brunel down and—urged the truth out of him. Oscar does not know that I know,' he added. 'I am keeping that piece of information to myself for a while longer.'

'Don't you dare hurt my father!' Mia flared up instantly.

Looking down at her, Nikos prompted dryly, 'Not hating him so much now?'

Mia shifted restlessly against him. 'I don't hate Oscar,' she admitted. 'I don't even hate my mother...' Her blue eyes shadowed over on the hollow ache she experienced. 'I was hurting when I said all of those things in the car. Oscar has been good to me—kind, even when my arrival caused him so much trouble.'

'Trouble you had a right to cause, Mia.'

'That's what he said to me,' she whispered, feeling guilty now that she had maligned the man who'd tried his very best to make her feel welcome and wanted. 'So,' she said, 'what was Oscar planning for you and me?'

'Oh, the full works, I should imagine.' Nikos smiled ruefully. 'Throw you in my way every damn day. Wind me up with some macho protectiveness and jealousy to aim me in the direction he wanted me to go.'

'Which was where?'

'White lace and wedding bells,' he enlightened. 'But without the premature baby conception… I will have let him down there.'

'You did not do so on your own,' Mia pointed out. 'I helped—a lot.'

At last she made his strained mouth stretch into a real proper grin. Reaching up she traced that wide warm mouth with a finger. 'You know what you need,' she ventured softly, long black eyelashes hiding away the sparkle in her blue eyes. 'You need a trial run sleeping with me in a bed for a whole night or two. I can live with no locks on the doors but I refuse to marry a man who insists on separate bedrooms because he thinks I will scare him into nightmares...'

The way she put the last part froze Nikos for a second or two before he threw back his dark head and laughed. Then with a groan he crushed her up against him, and claimed the pouting invitation of her lush mouth.

'Trial run coming up,' he muttered a while later. 'We will call Oscar tomorrow,' he planned as he drew towards her bed. 'If he doesn't threaten to kill me for seducing his daughter, he can give you away at our wedding.'

'And if he does threaten to kill you?' Mia ran a possessive hand down the front of his body and watched him shudder.

'I will warn him he will be making his daughter a widow because I'm still marrying you.'

It was gruff and strong and very possessive, and Mia curved her body in even closer. 'I love you, Nikos Theakis,' she told him.

'Well, keep on loving me, *agape mou*,' he responded unsteadily. 'I am about to risk dropping every protective guard I have in favour of loving you back by return.'

He had said it—almost said it. Mia laughed in delight. Then, with more strength than she gave credence to, she twisted him around and tumbled them both down on the bed.

'Show me, then,' she invited.

Nikos did not need telling twice.

Two wonderful months later, Nikos strode into the bedroom he'd had refurbished to accommodate his wife's *hobby*, as she liked to call it. Every one of their homes now had similar rooms, laid out like a fashion designer's studio with all the time-saving gadgets known to the trade.

'You're supposed to be dressed by now—' he frowned at Mia '—Santino and Nina D'Lassio will be here in half an hour and Tia Giulia is already downstairs with Oscar.'

'Is it that late?' Looking up from what she was doing, Mia felt the usual crash and burn take place inside her because he looked so deliciously gorgeous in a dinner suit—and, she tagged on possessively, every single bit of him belonged to her.

'You are not wearing that,' he said, his frown deepening as he spied the dress she had left hanging on an otherwise empty rail.

'Oh, you don't like it,' Mia murmured in disappointment.

'Are you joking?' Striding over to the bright red slip of silk and plucking up the hanger so he could view it more thoroughly, he said, 'It's a Jessica Rabbit dress.'

'Jessica who?' Mia asked innocently.

'Jessica Rabbit—the cartoon sex bomb and fantasy lover of every man with a healthy sex drive.'

Pleased by that remark, Mia stood to reveal the gold silk under the slip she was wearing. 'That's OK, then,' she said with relief.

'You're still not wearing it, Mia,' Nikos said firmly. 'Not in front of anyone but me anyway…'

'But you just said it was every man's fantasy!' Taking it from him she placed the hanger back on the rail again. Then, because she knew he was trying to work out how the heck he was going to stop her when she usually ended up doing as she pleased anyway, she turned to send him a grin.

'It's for Sophie,' she confided.

'Sophie—?' Nikos almost choked on the shock.

'She asked me to make her a really sexy dress,' she explained. 'And you have just made my day by telling me I have achieved the ultimate.'

'But—*agape mou*, you can't put Sophie in a dress like that! She's—'

'Don't you *dare* finish what you were about to say!' Mia flared up in heated defence of her half-sister. 'She is beautiful and nice!'

'I was not about to—'

'And she owns the most exquisite pocket Venus figure underneath those dreadful concealing garments she prefers to wear,' Mia cut in furiously. 'So she does not parade her figure as she should do, but that doesn't mean she cannot be encouraged.'

Absolutely not believing her but willing to accept he had just deeply offended his new wife on Sophie Balfour's behalf, Nikos went for the diversion. 'You're so sexy when you're sparked up and angry,' he murmured, reaching out to draw her into his embrace.

'Mmm, and you are one amazing kisser, *signor,*' she sighed out when he finally let her up for air.

'You've got no one else to compare me with,' Nikos pointed out.

'And you like to feel smug about that?'

'Sì, signora.' He grinned. 'I love it that you love me, and that I am the only man to kiss you, and that this hiding in here—' he moulded his hand to her still-flat stomach '—bears the fruits of my kisses and—other things.'

'That is just so—so old-fashioned and possessively Greek!' Mia frowned at him.

'But you love me to be old-fashioned and possessive.'

'I also think you should know that over

there—' she pointed to another rail packed with clothes '—is another Jessica Rabbit dress, as you call it, just waiting for me to put on if you don't watch your step!'

Caught like a rat in a trap, Mia watched his smile disappear and his eyes narrow to scan the indicated rail. 'I will burn it.'

'Before or after you see me wearing it?'

He took a minute to think about that, then he responded with a lusty growl, 'Afterwards. Private viewing.' He captured her already kiss-blushed lips.

'So what are you planning to wear?' he demanded long minutes later.

'You,' Mia whispered. 'Later,' she added in a soft invitation. 'In our bed, where it is my solemn duty to keep scaring your nightmares away.'

Nikos could have taken objection to her remarking on the nightmares, but he no longer hid anything from this beautiful creature he had won as his wife. It was healthier to keep everything—good or bad—right out there in the open.

'You know, I believed my life was all mapped out,' he confided softly. 'No U-turns, no diversions, just me in absolute control of me. Then I met you,' he husked. 'I did not want love. I did not want commitment. I did not want to pass on my family genes to another generation. Or to watch my children's disappointment in me grow each time I did not come up to scratch as a father. Now I want it all.' His fingers framed her upturned face, his eyes so dark Mia smiled because she just loved to drown in them. 'I want the marriage, the commitment and the children. I want you to love me. I *need* you to love me. It's crazy, frightening.'

'I'm not going anywhere,' Mia promised. Then, to lighten the sudden intense atmosphere, she begged, 'Just one more tiny kiss before I go and dress.'

Flat black eyebrows rose in disdain. 'I don't do tiny,' Nikos drawled arrogantly.

MORE ABOUT THIS BOOK

MORE ABOUT THE AUTHOR

THE BALFOUR BRIDES

Too Beautiful, Too Rich, Too Pampered...

Sisters synonymous with style, glamour and now scandal, the Balfour sisters have some hard lessons to learn...

The Balfour dynasty needs urgent help to save their reputations and show the world what they are worth:

The Father

Oscar Balfour must somehow make his daughters appreciate their charmed lives. Will they learn from his mistakes in love?

The Daughters

Eight sisters by four different mothers. Each must take a new direction in life to find out who she really is.

The Rules

Passed down through generations, the Balfour Family Rules offer the guidance Oscar's daughters desperately need.

Read on to discover more!

THE BALFOUR DYNASTY

The Balfour Family

The Balfour girls are a British institution, the last of the society heiresses. Oscar's daughters have grown up in the limelight and the Balfour name is rarely out of the tabloid newspapers. Having eight very different daughters is not without its challenges.

Olivia and Bella: Oscar's eldest daughters are non-identical twins, born two minutes apart, and couldn't be more different. Where Bella is wild and exuberant, Olivia is practical and sensible. Olivia's maturity is matched only by Bella's sense of fun and both twins epitomise key Balfour qualities. The death of their mother when they were young still affects them, although they show their feelings in very different ways!

Zoe: The youngest daughter of Oscar's first wife, Alexandra, who tragically died giving birth to her. Like her elder sister Bella, Zoe has a tendency to walk on the wild side and is forever looking for her next social engagement. Her looks are striking, with her green eyes setting her apart from her sisters, but behind her glamorous façade hides a good heart and guilt over her mother's death.

Annie: As the eldest of Oscar and Tilly's daughters, Annie has acquired a good business brain and a kind-hearted and practical outlook on life. Enjoying spending time with her mother at the Balfour estate, she has eschewed the glitterati lifestyle and concentrated more on her Oxford education than her looks.

Sophie: The middle child is usually the

quietest and Sophie Balfour is no exception. In comparison with her dazzling sisters, Sophie has always felt overlooked and is uncomfortable with being 'a Balfour girl'! Despite her shyness Sophie is artistically talented and has hidden passions that manifest themselves in her creative interior designs.

Kat: The youngest of Tilly's daughters has been wrapped in cotton wool her entire life. Since the tragedy of her step-father's death, she has been fussed over and compensated for by everyone. Her wilful and spoilt behaviour make her born to run from tough situations and she is adamant that she will never commit to anything or anyone!

Mia: The most recent addition to the Balfour family comes in the shape of Oscar's illegitimate, half-Italian daughter Mia. Born after a one-night stand between her mother and the head of the Balfour clan, Mia was raised in Italy and is hard-working, humble and naturally beautiful. Discovering her new family has been tough for Mia, the social poise of her blue-blooded sisters is difficult to master!

Emily: The youngest of Oscar's daughters and the only child of his one true love, Lillian. As the baby of the family Emily is adored by her older sisters, claims the favourite spot in her father's heart and has always been well protected. Unlike Kat, Emily remains down-to-earth and determined to make her dream of being a prima ballerina come true. The combined pressures of her mother's death and the revelation of Mia as her new sister take their toll on Emily and she has enough strength to leave her father's house and strike out on her own.

THE BALFOUR ESTATE

The Balfour family's property portfolio is extensive, covering several stunning residences in the most exclusive areas of London, a breathtaking apartment on New York's Upper East Side, a chalet in Klosters and a private holiday island in the Caribbean which is always in high demand with celebrities…although Oscar is very choosy about who can hire his retreat – no Z-list celebrities allowed!

However, the family seat is Balfour Manor, nestled in the heart of the Buckinghamshire countryside. It is this house that the girls all call home. With such a disrupted family life, this is the one place that represents security to each of them. It is here that the family spend Christmas together and, of course, they all gather again for the Balfour Charity Ball – the event of the year, attended by the *crème de la crème* of glittering society, in the heavenly setting of the gardens of the Balfour Manor.

LETTER FROM OSCAR BALFOUR TO HIS DAUGHTERS...

To my dear girls,

At best I have been an inattentive father to you all and it has taken recent tragic events to open my eyes to the trouble such carelessness has caused.

Our old family motto was 'Validus, Superbus quod Fidelis', or 'Powerful, Proud and Loyal'. By enforcing the ten principles above, I begin to make amends; not only will I endeavour to find these qualities in myself, I pray that you girls will do the same. Over the next few months, I shall expect all of you to take these rules to heart, for each and every one of you needs the guidance they contain. The tasks I shall set you and the journeys I shall send you upon aim only to help you to find yourselves – to achieve change, to develop and learn how to become the strong women you have it within yourselves to be.

Go forth, my beautiful daughters, and discover how each of your stories ends...

Oscar

THE BALFOUR FAMILY RULES

These ancient Balfour Rules have been passed down through the generations of the family. In the wake of the scandal revealed at the one hundredth Balfour Charity Ball, Oscar realised that his daughters lacked direction and clarity in their lives. Once discarded by Oscar, as a young and reckless man, the Family Rules were revived, revamped and re-instituted to offer the guidance his young daughters were in dire need of.

Rule 1 – Dignity: a Balfour must strive never to bring the family name into disrepute through unbecoming conduct, criminal activity or disrespectful attitudes towards others.

Rule 2 – Charity: the Balfours must not take for granted their vast family wealth. True riches are measured by how much one gives to others. Compassion is by far the most valuable possession.

Rule 3 – Loyalty: you owe loyalty to your siblings; treat them with respect and kindness at all times.

Rule 4 – Independence: members of the Balfour family must strive to achieve their own personal development and not rely on the family name to get them through life.

Rule 5 – Courage: a Balfour should be frightened of nothing. Face your fears with courage and they will lead to further self-discovery.

Rule 6 – Commitment: run away from your problems once and you will run forever.

Rule 7 – Integrity: don't be afraid to adhere to your principles and have faith in your own convictions.

Rule 8 – Humility: there is great strength in admitting your weaknesses and working to overcome them. Do not discard another's point of view merely because it does not agree with your own. A true Balfour can accept advice as well as offer it.

Rule 9 – Wisdom: do not judge appearances. True beauty lies beneath the skin. Honesty and integrity are worth far more than simple surface charm.

Rule 10 – The Balfour Name: being a family member is not merely a privilege of birth. The Balfour name entails supporting one another, valuing your family as you value yourself and carrying the Balfour name with pride. To deny your heritage is to deny your very essence.

MORE ABOUT THE AUTHOR: MICHELLE REID

Reading has been an important part of Michelle Reid's life as far back as she can remember and was encouraged by her mother, who made the twice-weekly bus trip to the nearest library to keep feeding this particular hunger in all five of her children. In fact, one of Michelle's most abiding memories from those days is coming home from school to find a newly borrowed selection of books stacked on the kitchen table just waiting to be delved into.

There has not been a day since that she hasn't had at least two books lying open somewhere in the house ready to pick up and continue whenever she has a quiet moment.

Her love of romantic fiction has always been strong, though she feels she was quite late in discovering the riches Mills & Boon has to offer. It wasn't long after making this discovery that she made the daring decision to try her hand at writing a romance for herself, never expecting it to become such an important part of her life.

Now she shares her time between her large, close, lively family and writing. She lives with her husband in a tiny white stone cottage in the English Lake District. It is both a romantic haven and the perfect base to go walking through some of the most beautiful scenery in England.

AN INTERVIEW WITH MICHELLE REID

What did you enjoy about writing a continuity title?

This was my first attempt at writing for a continuity series and I enjoyed the challenge of creating a story from someone else's ideas. However, the real challenge for me had to be disciplining myself to keep the story within continuity guidelines when my writer's head wanted to shoot off in all different directions!

Did you identify with the Balfour sister you were writing about?

Oh gosh, no. Mia Balfour was born and brought up in Italy, so I had to teach myself to think like an Italian heroine! I do this all the time with my Italian heroes but it felt somehow quite different climbing into the head of an Italian heroine. And Mia was so young and sweet and vulnerable and brave, I admired her from the beginning and I loved "learning" to understand her.

Which sister's hero did you find most appealing?

Besides Mia's hero, Nikos Theakis? I thought long and hard about this question but each time I decided on an answer I instantly changed my mind. So I suppose I have to say that I found them all appealing!

What do you think makes a great hero/ heroine?

Because our heroes are so strong, a great heroine must be able to stand up for her-self even when feeling desperately vulnerable. Likewise our forceful heroes must be in touch with their softer side around our heroines, no matter how tough and passionate their conflicts are. It's a kind of essential balance.

When you are writing, what is a typical day?

Usually I wake up each morning with a new scene buzzing inside my head, so my first priority (with a cup of coffee!) is to get that scene down fast, in case I lose it. Then I set to and read through what I've written the day before. I tweak, if it needs it, and sometimes fight with it because it wasn't doing what I had intended it to do. I like to leave the previous day's work with an unfinished sentence or a couple of word bites to remind me how I want to move the story on. Lunch is quick, a slice of toast and a glass of fresh juice, then the real work begins. If I'm working well I will write without noticing the hours passing by, until my neglected husband dares enter the lion's den (my office) and make rumbling noises about dinner.

If things are not going well I will break off halfway through the afternoon to do something really mindless like shopping or ironing, but I often have to race back to my computer halfway through because a solution to the problem I was struggling with has appeared out of nowhere! If the story is really grabbing hold of me I will work again after dinner and late into the night. I confess, the story rules me, not the other way around!

Feisty Kat Balfour has been sent to Carlos Guerrero's yacht. It's only when she's handed an apron that she realises she's there to *work*, not play. Brilliant businessman and thrill-seeking dare-devil, Carlos is an enigma. Trapped in the middle of the ocean with the most fiercely sexy and powerful man she has ever met, Kat is way out of her depth!

Carlos is amused by his new housekeeper – he'll put her to work, but he'd rather put her to bed! First he must tame the wilful beauty…

KAT'S PRIDE

The room in which she now stood was the polar opposite of the poky cabin she'd just been shown. This had the enormous dimensions she was used to – a grand dining salon set out on almost palatial lines. Inlaid lights twinkled from the ceiling – but these were eclipsed by the blaze of natural light which flooded in through sliding French windows which opened up onto the deck itself.

There was a dining table which would have comfortably seated twelve people, though Kat noticed that only two places had been laid and used. Various open bottles were lined along the gleaming surface and candle wax had dripped all over a bone-china plate. At its centre was a beautiful blue-glass platter of exotic fruits and next to it sat a crystal goblet of flat champagne, along with a carelessly abandoned chocolate wrapper.

Kat's lips pursed into a disapproving circle – wondering why on earth a member of staff hadn't bothered to clear it away. "What a disgusting mess," she observed quietly

"Isn't it?" agreed Mike, laughing. "The boss sure likes to party when he parties!"

So at least she now knew that the "boss" was a man. And an untidy man, by the look of things.

With a sudden smooth purring of powerful engines, the boat began to move – and Kat's eyes widened in surprise. But before she could register her inexplicable panic that they were setting sail so soon, something happened to wipe every thought clean from her mind.

The first was the sight of a bikini top – a flimsy little excuse for a garment in a shimmering gold material which was lying in a discarded heap on the polished oak floor. It was a blatant symbol of decadence and sex and, for a couple of seconds, the blood rushed hotly into her cheeks before she allowed herself to concentrate on the second.

Because the second was a photo of a man.

Kat's heart thundered as she stared at it, recognition hit her like a short sharp slap to the face.

The man in the photo must have been barely out of his teens, yet already his face was sombre and hardened by experience. Black eyes stared defiantly straight into the lens of the camera and his sensual lips curved in an expression which was undeniably formidable.

He was wearing a lavishly embroidered, glittering jacket, skin-tight trousers and some kind of dark and formal hat. It was an image which was unfamiliar and yet instantly recognisable and it took a few moments for Kat to realise that this was the traditional garb of the bullfighter. But that realisation seemed barely relevant in the light of the horror which was slowly beginning to dawn on her.

That she was staring at a likeness of the young Carlos Guerrero.

Trying to conceal the shaking of her hands, she turned to Mike.

"Whose boat is this?" she croaked.

Mike's blond head was jerked in the direction of the photo, and he smiled. "His."

"C-Carlos?" Even saying his name sent shivers down her spine – just as the memory of his harsh words lancing through her still had the power to wound. "Carlos Guerrero?"

"Sure. Who else?" Mike's expression grew even more curious. "You didn't know?"

Of course she didn't know! If she had known then she would never have set foot on the damned vessel – why, she wouldn't have gone within a million miles of it! But there was no way she was going to enlighten this smirking engineer about her misgivings, or the reason for them. She needed to assert her authority and get onto dry land again.

"I think there's been some kind of mix-up," she said, her smooth tone belying the fast beating of her heart and sudden sense of urgency. "And I'd like to go ashore. Please."

"I'm afraid that won't be possible."

Kat's eyes narrowed. "What are you talking about?"

"Well, Carlos told me that a new domestic was arriving – and that her name was Kat Balfour."

One word reverberated around the room and she repeated it, just in case she had mis-heard it. "Domestic?" she repeated incredulously.

"Sure. You're Kat Balfour and there's six hungry crew on board." He smiled. "And we need someone to clean up after us and make our meals, don't we?"

It was so outrageous a statement to make, that for a moment Kat thought he must be having some kind of – extremely unfunny – joke at her expense. As if she was some kind of lowly deck-hand who was about to wait on a load of crew members! But one look at his face told her he was deadly serious. What the *hell* was going on?

© Harlequin Books SA 2010.
With special thanks and acknowledgement to
Sharon Kendrick

THE

Balfour

LEGACY

EIGHT SISTERS, EIGHT SCANDALS

Volume 2

Kat's Pride by Sharon Kendrick

Available 16th July 2010